Sweet Dreams

ETERNAL REST
BED AND BREAKFAST

PARANORMAL COZY MYSTERIES

BETH DOLGNER

Sweet Dreams
Eternal Rest Bed and Breakfast Book One
© 2021 Beth Dolgner

ISBN-13: 978-1-7365724-2-9

Sweet Dreams is a work of fiction. Names, characters, places, and incidents either are the products of the author's imagination or are used fictitiously. Any resemblance to actual persons, living or dead, businesses, companies, events, or locales is entirely coincidental.

Published by Redglare Press
Cover by Dark Mojo Designs
Print Formatting by The Madd Formatter

BethDolgner.com

Dedicated to David Moore,
in celebration of his retirement from Historic Oakland Foundation.
Thank you for your dedicated stewardship of the cemetery that
inspired this novel.

Emily balanced the tray in one hand as she put the other against the dining room door. Before she could push it open, she heard a gasp and a woman's nervous giggle. Smiling, Emily glanced at the chocolate chip cookies piled on the tray. They were fresh out of the oven, but they could wait. Whether or not something paranormal was happening in the dining room, she didn't want to break her guests' concentration.

Sage's low, sonorous voice drifted into the hallway as Emily turned and walked quietly back to the kitchen. On the rare occasions there was an extra place at the table, Emily would join in the monthly séance. As usual, though, the Spirited Saturday Night package at Eternal Rest Bed and Breakfast was sold out. People came from all over the country for the chance to spend the weekend with ghosts.

Emily put the tray down on the small wooden table shoved into one corner of the kitchen. All of the appliances were modern, but this little table was an antique that had been in the house for decades. She sat down with a satisfied sigh, then shrugged and picked up a cookie. *Someone should enjoy them while they're warm*, she thought. Emily stretched her legs out in front of her and kicked off her shoes. A quiet moment like this was rare on these weekends. Spirited Saturday Night guests started arriving at lunchtime on Friday and stayed through Sunday morning. On Friday night, Emily would host a welcome reception, where the guests drank cocktails with spooky names and listened to Emily's stories about the Victorian house's history as a home to both the living and the dead. Emily's best friend, Sage Clark, took over on Saturday night, treating everyone to a séance. Sometimes there wasn't much paranormal activity, but there was always something. Emily had been skeptical about psychics when she first met Sage, but after years of seeing her in action, Emily was a believer—in Sage's abilities, at least. She still inwardly scoffed at some of the ridiculous claims made by other psychic mediums who came to stay at Eternal Rest.

With a sigh, Emily wiped a few crumbs from her lips and stood up. If she got the coffee maker ready to go for tomorrow, then she could simply flip the switch in the morning to get it going in time for breakfast. The dishwasher needed to be unloaded, too, and the garbage was full. And when she took the garbage bag out to the bin, Emily could grab the watering can and get the plants watered while she was out there. It had been an unusually warm day for this early in March.

Emily allowed herself a few moments of self-pity while she slipped on her shoes again. Running a bed and breakfast in this house had always been her dream. Doing it all by herself had never been part of the plan.

About half an hour later, just as Emily had relaxed into the kitchen chair again, she heard the dining room door squeak open and footsteps in the hallway. When she went out to greet her guests, everyone was smiling.

"You should have been there!" exclaimed one of the men. "There were knocking noises!"

Emily smiled and offered her best effort at surprise. "That's fantastic!"

"It was so exciting," added his wife. "And Sage, oh, what a talented medium she is. You, my dear, have a very crowded house, even if you can't see most of the inhabitants!"

Emily glanced past the guests to catch Sage's eye, and they exchanged gratified smiles. A successful séance always meant good reviews on the online travel sites, and it often-times meant guests would come back again to experience more. After staying in a haunted bed and breakfast, going back to staying in ordinary hotels was just too boring for some people.

The four couples drifted up the stairs to their rooms, calling good night to Emily and Sage while still giggling and talking with each other.

"They were easily impressed," Emily said quietly once the final set of feet had reached the second-floor landing.

"People usually are," Sage agreed. "For people who don't normally witness any kind of paranormal activity, even the smallest thing is thrilling." Sage was still smiling, dimples showing in her round face. She absent-mindedly fingered the ankh pendant hanging around her neck, and her eyelids drooped. Her eyes seemed to be fixed on a spot on the wall, but Emily knew it was the face Sage made when she was trying to channel a message from a spirit.

"You made cookies," Sage said abruptly.

"Did a spirit just bother to show up and tell you that?"

Sage laughed. "I could smell them earlier. I hope you didn't eat them all yourself."

"Come on; they're in the kitchen." Emily led her back there, gesturing to the table while she automatically pulled a bottle of cabernet off the white granite countertop. As she poured, she cleared her throat. "So, did he come by tonight?" She tried to make it sound casual, as always, but it still sounded desperate to her ears.

"Em, honey, you know he didn't." Even with her back

to Sage, Emily could tell her friend's smile was gone. "If Scott ever showed up, I would tell you immediately."

"I know." Emily jammed the cork back into the bottle and carried the two glasses over to the table. "And you know I have to ask."

Sage picked up her glass and raised it in a toast. "Your husband loved you, and you loved him. I doubt he had any unfinished business. I say this to you every month, but there is no reason for his spirit to still be on this plane. But, like every month, here's to his memory." Sage clinked her glass against Emily's.

After taking a long sip, the edges of Sage's mouth turned up again. "Mrs. Thompson stopped by tonight. Bless her heart, she refuses to accept the fact that she's dead. She thinks she still works for you."

"I wish I had the ability to communicate with spirits like you. Mrs. Thompson always had the best town gossip to share. I bet she has even more now that she's a ghost and can eavesdrop on everyone." Emily had been fond of the elderly woman, a retired widow who had come to work at Eternal Rest two days a week, which gave Emily the chance to run errands and occasionally meet up with friends. "She's been gone for five months already. I wonder when she'll finally cross over."

"I gave her a little prod in the right direction, but it might take her a while to get there. She was a stubborn old lady."

"Sage!"

"Oh, I'm not disrespecting the dead. It's just the truth." Sage pointed toward the ceiling, as if Mrs. Thompson was hovering above them. "She knows what I think. I told her so when she was alive, and I told her again tonight."

The two women chatted until their wine glasses were empty. Sage covered her mouth as she yawned. "Wow, the spirits took it out of me tonight. Time to head home. I'll see you tomorrow afternoon for coffee, right?"

Emily gave a mock salute as she rose. "I'll be there."

It was still a comfortable temperature outside. As Emily walked Sage across the front porch, which spanned the entire width of the house, a soft breeze promised that spring was on the way. Emily took a deep breath, smelling the dogwood blossoms that were just appearing on the trees that flanked the brick stairs leading up to the porch. The white flowers always looked so pretty against the dark-blue exterior of the house. Sage paused suddenly and turned to her left, looking in the direction of the cemetery that sat next to the house. The golden glow of the porch light made it impossible to see the cemetery in the darkness beyond, but its invisible presence could still be felt.

Sage was motionless for a long time, her eyes again taking on their half-lidded look. As the silence dragged on, the breeze suddenly felt cold to Emily, and a little shiver worked its way from the base of her spine up to her neck. Finally, unable to stand the suspense, Emily whispered, "What?"

Sage shook her head, as if she were forcing herself to refocus. Her voice had just a tinge of worry. "I don't know." When she caught Emily's concerned look, she reached out and squeezed her arm. "Nothing to worry about. Sometimes other entities are drawn to the séances, but usually they're too weak to communicate anything. Well, good night, Em. See you tomorrow!"

Emily stayed on the porch as she watched Sage get into her car and drive away, trying to sense whatever had caught Sage's attention, but all she felt was the night air. Finally, with one last shiver, Emily went back inside, locking the heavy wooden door behind her.

There were a few empty glasses in the dining room, so

Emily stacked them and took them back to the kitchen. She returned to put down the place settings for breakfast the next morning, then walked across the hall to check the parlor for any stray glasses. Like the dining room, the parlor was spacious and had windows on two walls. The windows in the wall facing the front porch stretched all the way from the floor to the ceiling. During nice spring and fall weather, the open windows gave guests easy access to the porch. North Georgia summers were too hot for that, and Emily was glad her grandparents had retrofitted the house with a very modern air-conditioning system. It still got stuffy on the third floor, but that gabled room was only used for storage now, anyway.

Finally done for the night, Emily double-checked that all of the lights were off and retreated into her bedroom, which was at the back of the ground floor, across the hall from the kitchen. The same breeze that had felt so good on the porch was now blowing through the open bedroom window. Not wanting to get a chill in the middle of the night, though, Emily shut it, but not before gazing toward the cemetery. The first headstones were only two-hundred feet away, and here at the back of the house, where the light from the porch didn't reach, they stood out gray against the darkness. People who didn't know Emily well always expressed shock when they learned her bedroom had a cemetery view, but Emily loved beginning and ending each day with the historic property. Yes, the house and cemetery grounds were haunted, but she had never experienced anything more uncomfortable than the flirta-tious ghost of Mr. Dawson, who liked to personally welcome women to his mausoleum. And if there had been a truly evil entity lurking there, Emily was certain that Sage would have sensed it by now and given her a warning.

Emily's mind immediately went back to Sage's behavior on the front porch. She had definitely been

sensing something unusual from the direction of the cemetery, and despite her words of reassurance, Emily couldn't
help but wonder what exactly Sage had perceived. Or
maybe, thought Emily, the question wasn't what, but
whom.

2

Not bothering to close the curtains, Emily quickly changed into her pajamas and slid into bed. The sturdy mahogany bed frame was at least a century old, too heavy for Emily to move by herself and far too big for just one person. The room had the same high ceiling as the rest of the house, but instead of putting up cheerful wallpaper like the guest rooms had, Emily had opted for a more modern look of pale-gray paint. The wardrobe and vanity were antiques, though, and the bathroom that had been shoe-horned into one corner during the house's renovation into a bed and breakfast included an old claw-foot porcelain bathtub. Emily loved telling guests that when the house was built in 1872, there was no full bathroom. Victorian ladies would have used a chamber pot indoors or an outhouse in the backyard. "Imagine trying to manage that in a corset and bustle!" Emily would always say in conclusion.

Emily turned off the bedside lamp and felt her body relax. Some of the guests were still awake, and she could hear the wooden floors above her creaking slightly. She drifted off to sleep as the house gradually quieted down.

The sun was just peeking over the horizon when Emily woke up the next morning. She started the coffee maker before taking a quick shower and pulling on her usual black jeans and blue button-down shirt that had *Eternal Rest*

Bed and Breakfast embroidered in silver on the left breast. She pulled her light-brown hair into a high ponytail, then twisted it into a tight knot. Lip balm and a quick dusting of powder were as much as she had time for before heading back to the kitchen to start warming up the croissants, danishes, and bagels. The bakery delivered them every afternoon when she had guests, and Emily nibbled on a croissant as she worked.

As she was arranging a tray of cold deli meats and sliced cheeses to go with the baked goods, there was a quiet knock at the back door. Emily knew who it was even before she opened it to see a tall man with smooth brown skin and dark eyes that looked like they were laughing at an inside joke. He was wearing a tailored three-piece suit of dark-gray wool.

Emily waved Reed in, skipping a greeting and diving in with, "You always show up right as I'm getting breakfast ready."

"A coincidence, I assure you," Reed said with a wink. "I just like coming out here early on Sunday mornings to visit the family." Still, he happily accepted the plate that Emily now handed him. As he sat down at the kitchen table, Emily noticed he had a small cardboard box in his hand.

"The latest finds?" Emily nodded toward the box as she scooped butter onto a serving dish.

"Just a few things, mostly from the work over at the Clements plot." Reed Marshall was the sexton at the town's modern cemetery, Oak Hill Memorial Garden, but the historic Hilltop Cemetery adjacent to Eternal Rest was under his care, as well. The land had belonged to Emily's family for about half a century, but the graves and monuments themselves were maintained by the city of Oak Hill. Since Oak Hill was a small town, there were only a few burials at the Memorial Garden each week. That meant

Reed and his team were easily able to balance taking care of both cemeteries.

Currently, Reed and his team were rebuilding a low brick wall surrounding the Clements plot. Over the years, shifting ground and plant roots had caused two of its four sides to collapse. The team was removing all of the bricks so that a new, flat foundation could be laid before reconstruction began. Reed was constantly finding things on the cemetery grounds, from old objects that turned up during renovations and maintenance to items accidentally left behind by tourists. Usually, it was a collection of sunglasses and coins.

Emily reached over and lifted the box, giving it a gentle shake. "Hmm, I'm going to guess there are fifty-three cents in here. I'm going to be rich!" She slid the box onto the top of the microwave and returned her attention to breakfast.

At the sound of footsteps on the stairs, Emily swept both trays up and hustled toward the dining room, hoping to beat her guests there. "I'll be back!" she called to Reed as she disappeared into the hallway.

"Nah, I'm off to see the family," he responded. "If the croissants are leaving, then so should I."

Emily rolled her eyes even though Reed couldn't see her, but she was smiling. The care he gave to Hilltop Cemetery definitely earned him breakfast now and then. He was probably the only person in town who was as sentimental about the cemetery as Emily. It wasn't just because it was Reed's job to care about the cemetery. His great-great-grandfather had been the first African-American to be buried at Hilltop. Reed lovingly tended the plot personally, and he was always eager to tell any visitors who happened to stroll by about his family's roots in Oak Hill.

The couple who had been so complimentary of Sage the night before was already at the foot of the stairs. Emily was always surprised how early some people liked to rise on what was supposed to be a relaxing weekend. It was barely after seven. Emily wished them a good morning and nodded to the trays she was carrying. "Follow me!"

Emily put the trays down and went back to the kitchen for the carafe of coffee. When she reentered the dining room, the couple—from Kentucky, Emily remembered— were bent over an old book that Emily recognized as one that normally adorned the nightstand in their room. The woman was pointing at a map printed on one of the pages. She looked up as Emily poured coffee for them. "We want to go here today," she stated.

"And where is 'here'?"

"This old mill down by Tanner's Creek. Do you know if any of it still exists? We like hiking, and Tim loves fall-ing-apart old buildings."

"Sure. A couple of the brick buildings are still there, but you can't go in them," said Emily. "They say it's haunted, you know. People hear the sounds of children playing inside, but all of the windows and doors are boarded up. There's no way anyone can be in there, so it must be ghosts making the noises."

"Have you heard the sounds?"

"Oh, no. I haven't even been out there in years. I spend most of my time with the ghosts here."

"So…" The woman hesitated and looked at her husband expectantly.

"So," Tim echoed her, "we were wondering if Rhonda and I can stay another night. I can get the day off tomor-row, so we can go explore today and drive home on Monday."

Emily forced herself to smile. "Of course! I'd love to have you two for another night!" Inwardly, she was disap-pointed. Yes, the additional money would be welcome. There were some repairs the house needed—there was always something that needed to be fixed in an old house like hers—and every penny helped. At the same time, though, that meant Emily would be stuck at the house all day because she would need to be there when they returned, whenever that might be. No running errands, no meeting Sage at the café and, possibly worst of all, no lazy Sunday afternoon nap. Sunday afternoons were usually Emily's favorite part of the week: after weekend guests checked out, she would clean up, ready the rooms for the next round of guests, then lounge on the sofa in the parlor with a book and an iced tea. A nap was always part of the ritual, too.

Rhonda and Tim were both grinning now, and after thanking Emily, they immediately launched into planning their excursion. Emily left them to it, retreating into the kitchen to call Sage and cancel their plans.

At least Rhonda and Tim turned out to be very gracious guests. They returned from the mill with a handful of wild-flowers they had picked for Emily. She arranged them in a vase and placed them on a small walnut side table in the parlor. Emily had spent the day cleaning the downstairs area. Whenever she had guests, she felt obligated to be at the house and available, just in case. When Mrs. Thompson had been alive and working at Eternal Rest, Emily had reveled in those two days of freedom. She had been trying to find a replacement since the week of Mrs. Thompson's funeral, but with no luck. Few people were looking for a job that was only two days a week, students couldn't take the job because it conflicted with school hours, and one retiree had expressed interest until realizing where exactly the job was. The man firmly declared he would never work in a haunted house, especially not one next to a cemetery.

Emily woke up sometime in the early morning hours on Monday. Since the other weekend guests had checked out, it was only Rhonda and Tim staying upstairs. Emily didn't know what had disturbed her sleep, but she had the distinct feeling it had been some kind of noise. She sat up in bed, listening closely, but she heard nothing. Then, softly, she heard footsteps on the second floor. Emily flopped back into bed and huffed out a breath. She used to sleep so well, but ever since Scott died, she had become overly sensitive to every little sound. If a guest trod across the creaky floorboards to visit the bathroom in the middle of the night, Emily would almost always wake up, sigh, and roll over. Some nights, she would hear noises even when she was the only person in the house.

In the weeks after Scott's death, Emily had hoped the night noises might be a sign that he was there with her. She would peer through the dark, looking for his familiar shape, and call his name softly. If his spirit had ever been present, though, it hadn't made itself known to Emily in the past two years of waiting and hoping.

Emily finally drifted off to sleep again, and even though dim morning light illuminated her bedroom the next time she woke up, it wasn't her alarm that had roused her. It was footsteps on the staircase and a raised woman's voice.

Instantly alert, Emily hastily got out of bed and dressed. She ran a hand through her hair as she hurried into the hall. She paused on the threshold of her bedroom, listening. The heavy steps and Rhonda's tone told her something was wrong, but that didn't mean Emily needed to involve herself in it. It didn't happen often, but sometimes guests would argue with each other, and Emily had learned to steer clear of a couple in a fight.

Tim's voice drifted down the hall from the staircase.

"Are you sure you left it on the dresser, though?" The forced patience in his tone was clear.

"Yes." Rhonda's voice, on the other hand, had a tinge of panic. "Besides, I looked everywhere else it could be: on the nightstand, on the floor, behind the dresser, in my suitcase, on my damn finger!" Now she was almost yelling.

Emily dashed into the kitchen and turned on the coffee maker. She was going to need a few cups this morning if she was going to have disgruntled guests to deal with.

"Are you missing something?" she called as she walked toward them. Emily stopped short when she saw Rhonda's face. It was streaked with tears, and she was chewing on her lip nervously.

"My ring. My grandmother's beautiful emerald ring. It's just gone." Rhonda's voice had sunk to a whisper now.

Emily gestured to the parlor. "Let's sit down. I heard you say it was on your dresser?"

Rhonda nodded as she and Tim perched on the edge of the sofa. "I wear it every day, but I don't sleep with it on. I put it on the dresser next to my watch when I went to bed, just like I did on Friday and Saturday. It's just gone. Someone must have stolen it."

"Rhonda…" her husband began.

"What else could have happened?" Rhonda's voice was rising again.

"I have security cameras," Emily offered. "One at the front door and one at the back. They record any movement, so we can check and see if anyone came in." No one had entered Eternal Rest during the night. Emily was certain of that. The sound would have woken her. Whenever the security cameras did detect movement, it was always raccoons and possums nosing around. Of course, there were the times when the cameras were activated, but there was nothing at all to see in the recording. Emily often wondered if spirits somehow triggered the motion sensors.

At that thought, she drew her eyebrows together and stared down at her hands. Had items ever gone missing before? Not that Emily could think of, but then again, maybe no guest had ever left such a pretty prize simply lying in the open like Rhonda had. She looked at Rhonda sheepishly. "I know this will sound ridiculous, but it's entirely possible that the thief isn't one we'll see on a camera."

Tim frowned, but Rhonda actually perked up. "You think a ghost stole my ring?"

Emily shrugged slightly. "It's possible. But, rest assured, whatever happened to your ring, it's still in this house somewhere. If you don't find it before you head home, I'll certainly keep an eye out for it. And I'll make sure to inspect every nook and cranny when I clean your room."

"If it was a ghost, maybe that explains my dream," Rhonda said abruptly.

Tim still looked unhappy, and he shook his head. "It was just a dream, like I told you when you woke me up at three in the morning."

The same time I woke up, Emily noted to herself. She gestured to Rhonda. "Tell me what you dreamed."

"I was outside, and it was nighttime. Someone grabbed me from behind and pinned my arms. I was trying to break free, but I couldn't. Then I heard a man say, 'You don't deserve this fancy jewelry!' I felt pressure against my neck, and I tried to scream, but nothing came out. That's when I woke up."

Emily looked at Rhonda thoughtfully. The woman certainly seemed sincere, and Emily didn't doubt she had really had this nightmare, but Emily wasn't convinced there was anything paranormal about it. After all, the ghosts at Eternal Rest weren't violent, and they never intentionally scared guests. "I can't say whether the two

15

events are related," Emily finally said. "However, like I said, I'm going to make my own search for the ring."

Rhonda seemed satisfied with this promise, but Tim looked skeptical. Emily got the impression that he believed Rhonda had simply misplaced the ring. "When you check out, I'll ask you to draw me a sketch of the ring so I know what I'm looking for," Emily continued. "In the meantime, would you like some breakfast? The coffee should be ready."

Tim shook his head. "No, I think we'll go ahead and hit the road. Thanks, though."

Emily watched them trudge back up the stairs to their room and sighed quietly. She hated the thought of guests leaving Eternal Rest feeling unhappy, especially when it was something beyond her ability to make right.

Rhonda and Tim checked out half an hour later, and Emily found herself apologizing to them even though the missing ring had nothing to do with her. Because it had happened under her roof, Emily felt like she was somehow responsible.

As soon as the couple had pulled out of the circular driveway and onto the two-lane road that led into downtown Oak Hill, Emily decided to get to work cleaning their room. The other rooms had been cleaned the day before, and if she could get this one done, then Emily would be ready for the next guests. A couple had booked a stay from Wednesday all the way through Sunday. The idea of having most of her Monday and all day Tuesday free and alone sounded glorious. Those rare guest-free days were even more precious now that Mrs. Thompson was gone.

Emily grabbed her bucket of cleaning supplies from the cabinet under the kitchen sink and walked up the stairs with determination. Since her day had gotten off to such an early start, she could be finished with everything before nine o'clock. With that goal in mind, Emily unlocked the door to the room that Rhonda and Tim had been staying in.

They had made a mess. The comforter and top sheet had been stripped off the bed, probably during their frantic search for the ring. Even the pillowcases had been removed, and Emily pictured Rhonda shaking them out in case the ring had mysteriously wound up inside one of them. The couple had at least made some effort to tidy up after themselves, piling the sheets and pillows in one corner of the room. Emily decided it was actually helpful to have all but the flat sheet already stripped off the bed.

The vintage photos and a vase of flowers had clearly been moved off the dresser, then replaced haphazardly, and one of the paintings on the wall—hills covered by trees with fall-hued leaves—was even askew. Rhonda and Tim had left no spot untouched.

Which is why Emily was astonished to see a little gold ring with a gleaming green emerald stone sitting right in the middle of the bed.

3

Emily gasped and shouted, "Thank you!" She wasn't even sure whom she was thanking, but it felt like the right response. She dropped the cleaning bucket and lunged forward to grab the ring, as if it might wink out of sight at any moment. Questions began running through her mind. Could Rhonda and Tim have possibly missed the ring even though it was sitting in plain sight? Had they left it there on purpose, setting this whole scenario up as some kind of joke or their own manufactured version of a ghost story? Had the ring really been stolen and then returned from some paranormal thief?

Grasping the ring tightly in one hand, Emily rushed downstairs to the parlor, where a small roll-top desk against one wall served as her office. She opened her laptop and brought up the contact information for the couple, then dialed the cell phone number Tim had provided. They couldn't be more than a few miles away.

Tim answered on the second ring, and Emily nearly shouted at him, "I have it! I found the ring!"

Ten minutes later, the ring was back on Rhonda's finger as she stood on the front porch, hugging Emily tightly. She kept repeating her thanks.

Emily gently extracted herself from the embrace.

"You're welcome, but I think whoever took it is to thank. It's like they wanted to return it."

"You really think it was a ghost?" Tim sounded a little less skeptical than he had that morning.

Emily looked at Rhonda, who was beaming even though her eyes shone with tears. No, Emily decided, they hadn't simply overlooked the ring or set this up. They had genuinely been haunted. "I really think so. I just don't know which of our ghosts would have done this. We've got a few ghosts who haunt this place, like Mrs. Thompson, of course, but none of them has ever stolen anything before. Maybe it was just too pretty for them to resist."

This time, Rhonda and Tim drove away happy, their earlier stress forgotten in their new excitement about having experienced more genuine paranormal activity. Emily, on the other hand, sat for a long time on the porch swing that hung in front of the parlor windows, lost in thought about her ghosts and wondering how well she really knew them.

Finally, with a shiver that Emily wasn't sure came from the cold or the idea of one of her ghosts stealing from her guests, she went back inside the house to finish cleaning Rhonda and Tim's room. Emily changed the sheets, dusted, and vacuumed while constantly looking over her shoulder. After living for ten years in that house without ever feeling afraid of its resident ghosts, Emily didn't like this new feeling of doubt. Not only was she uncomfortable about not having full trust in the ghosts of Eternal Rest, but she also didn't like thinking of the implications that paranormal activity like this might have on the living. She had gotten lucky today: the ring had reappeared, Rhonda and Tim were able to quickly retrieve it, and everything had a nice, neat ending. The next time might not be so simple.

If there is a next time, Emily reminded herself. *Just because it happens once, doesn't mean it's going to become a problem.*

With the cleaning done, Emily finally helped herself to breakfast. She had made a full carafe of coffee, expecting that Rhonda and Tim would want some, and she still had some baked goods left over from the bakery's delivery on Saturday. Emily usually sat in the kitchen to eat, but today she put everything on a tray and took it into the parlor. She sat in one of the wingback chairs, arranged the tray on a nearby Ottoman, and sat back with her cup of coffee.

Lounging in the parlor like this was both a blessing and a curse, Emily decided. The sun brightened the room, giving the antique furnishings a fresh-looking glow, but it also highlighted the light-brown water stains in one corner, where the wallpaper was barely clinging to the wall. The dark-green ferns printed on the cream wallpaper even looked a little wilted in that spot. Eternal Rest really needed a new roof, but that was out of Emily's budget after having to completely replace the plumbing in one of the guest rooms just six months ago. The roof leak had supposedly been patched, but the water stain looked a little bigger with every passing month.

Well, there was nothing she could do about it right now. Emily shifted her eyes away, focusing instead on the portrait of her grandparents, which hung between the front windows. It had been painted when they were in their sixties, so it was the version of them she had known as a child. They were the ones who had bought the house and converted it into a bed and breakfast, and Emily had only been twelve when she started talking about taking it over for them when they were finally ready to retire. Grandpa John had died only five years after Emily and Scott started running Eternal Rest, and Grandma Ellen had followed him a year after that. And then Scott had died, and Emily was left feeling like her loved ones were being taken away from her, one after the other. Sometimes she called her parents just to make sure they were still among the living.

Sage had said that Grandpa John and Grandma Ellen stopped by often to see how Emily was getting along. The telltale signs of their presence, Sage would tell her, were the scent of roses—Grandma Ellen had cultivated roses in the back flower bed, but they were now looking neglected —and the faint "foosh" sound of a hand running over an object. That, Sage would say, was Grandpa John checking surfaces like the dining room table or one of the mantel-pieces for dust. Even in the afterlife, he was still making sure Eternal Rest looked its best.

"Grandpa? Grandma?" Emily called to the empty parlor. "If y'all are here, will you tell the ghosts to please not steal things? I need happy guests so I can afford to get this roof fixed."

Emily paused, as if she expected a verbal answer, then rose, carefully picking up a few crumbs that had fallen onto the floor and putting them back on the tray. "And yes, I know, no one is supposed to eat in the parlor. I'm feeling rebellious today."

Sometimes it felt good to talk to her grandparents out loud, as if they were really there to listen to her complaints, her worries, and even her quiet tears when the house was empty and the loneliness seemed overbearing. Emily could feel it building now, a sort of weariness mixed with a feeling of never-ending change.

"Right. Time to get out for a bit," Emily announced. She glanced at her watch and realized she still had another hour before she and Sage had agreed to meet at the café to make up for their canceled Sunday plan. That meant there was time for a stroll around the cemetery. It was hard to be lonely there, Emily liked to tell herself, surrounded by more than three thousand people. Yes, they were dead, but they were still fun to visit.

Historic Hilltop Cemetery was sprawled across twenty acres of land right next to Eternal Rest. The focal point of the property was, just as the name so simply stated, the top of a gentle hill. The biggest, most expensive mausoleums were up there, since the elevation made the spot the best real estate in the cemetery. As one walked down the sides of the hill in either direction, the mausoleums grew smaller until they were finally completely replaced by headstones.

The widest paths through Hilltop Cemetery ran in concentric circles around the hill, and over the years locals had named each ring road after its notable features or the names of people buried alongside it. Emily's favorite walk was called Sailor's Loop, the fourth path from the top and named after a monument to a sailor who had been lost at sea. A giant mast had been carved from marble, along with an anchor and what looked like a billowing sail that was inscribed with the sailor's unhappy fate: *Frederick Mitchell, besieged by pirates and lost to sea, 1857-1879.* When she was younger, Emily would gleefully write stories about Frederick and the gruesome adventures she'd imagined for him. Now, she simply enjoyed the incredible artistry of the monument.

The oak and maple trees were still bare, waiting for spring to fully arrive, but the holly bushes and magnolia trees cast shadows over the ground with their dark-green leaves. The magnolias wouldn't bloom for another couple of months, an event that always marked the end of spring in Emily's mind. The dogwood blossoms declared the end of winter, and the magnolia trees ushered in the summer. Today was still that perfect early spring weather, which Georgia had far too little of every year. The air was crisp, and it was chilly in the shade but warm under the cloudless sky. Emily, wearing a bright-yellow cardigan to match the sun, stuck to the sunniest parts of the cemetery.

On the third path from the hilltop, Emily paused at the Clements plot. It was one of the plots she could see from the side windows of the house, but from that perspective it was hard to appreciate how much work had been done by Reed and his team. The overgrown plants and weeds had been removed, the bricks from the wall that lined the plot had all been neatly piled on one side, and the work had begun to remove the wall's original foundation.

The cemetery and the house had been purchased by Emily's grandparents nearly fifty years before. The two locations had always been considered a single entity since the house was originally built for the cemetery sexton and his family to live in. Emily sometimes teased Reed about not getting a house as a part of his job with the city of Oak Hill, but he assured Emily that he wanted a modern house and not a potential money pit. Considering the looming roof problem, Emily could understand his point.

That lonely feeling had followed Emily out to the cemetery. She waved a hand as if to ward it off and headed for her car. A latte and Sage's company would make her feel better.

The Depot was already crowded with people enjoying the final minutes of their lunch breaks when Emily arrived, but it was easy to spot Sage's bubblegum-pink spiked hair. She had already snagged a spot at one of the small tables outside. Emily thought The Depot was intended to look like a Parisian café, with its wicker-backed chairs and polished circular tables lining the front patio. It didn't really feel all that exotic, but they made good food and even better ice cream, so Emily wasn't going to complain about aesthetics. Besides, the café overlooked the town square, which provided a nice patch of green right in the middle of the historic downtown. Oak Hill had once been a thriving railroad town, though these days traffic into and out of the city mostly consisted of antiques-lovers in SUVs. Half of the shops on the square held some combination of genuine antiques and cheap, old junk.

Sage was eyeing Emily as she sat down at the table. "What?" Emily said self-consciously. "I've been out on the grounds; do I have leaves in my hair again?" Some embar-rassments were hard to forget, and the incident at a Christmas party a few years back was one of them.

"It's your aura."

There was concern in Sage's voice, but Emily nearly

laughed. "I don't need another thing to worry about, so you can keep your auras to yourself."

Sage leaned forward and put her hand over Emily's. "I'm serious. You're stuck in the past. With Scott. Sometimes you're here with us, in the present, but on days like today, you're in another time altogether."

Emily turned her hand over and squeezed Sage's fingers. She knew lying to her was no use. "The house felt really empty today, once the guests left." Emily suddenly sat up straight. "Oh!"

"Hey, there you are! Welcome to the present moment. What snapped you back into our reality?"

"The weirdest thing happened this morning!" Emily told Sage the full story of the emerald ring, then waited anxiously for her response. Instead, Sage simply gazed at her for a long moment.

"Well?" Emily prompted.

"I'm thinking back to Saturday night. I didn't sense anything unusual during the séance. It was the normal levels of paranormal activity—knocking, cold spots, things like that. Your resident ghosts don't seem like the types who would steal things."

"I thought the same."

Sage narrowed her eyes. "It could have been your guests themselves." When Emily started to object, Sage held up a hand to stop her. "I don't mean they faked it," she clarified. "Some people carry their hauntings with them. It can be an actual spirit, but usually it's energy. A poltergeist is typically attached to an older child, so wherever they go, the poltergeist activity follows. Maybe your guests have something similar going on. Maybe they had a fight, and the negative energy manifested itself physically. And sometimes old trauma can, well, leak out into the physical world. That sort of thing."

"They seemed like really nice people to me." Emily felt

slightly offended at the idea that her guests had anything negative attached to them.

"Me, too, but even nice people can carry negative energy around. Still, I feel like I would have sensed something off about them if that were the case. But, unless one of your docile ghosts has taken to stealing, that's the most likely explanation."

A server came to take their order then, and after Emily requested her usual latte and a bagel with cream cheese, she turned to Sage. "Thanks again for pushing this to today. I really need to get an assistant again so I can have more of a normal life."

"You will. And soon." Sage smiled knowingly. Her gaze suddenly looked at a point behind Emily. "Trevor Williams!" she boomed.

Emily turned to see an attractive, tanned man with bright-blue eyes staring at them. He looked startled to hear his name, but he soon smiled. It made him even more handsome, Emily thought. Trevor approached their table in two quick strides. Emily vaguely remembered him from high school, but she certainly hadn't remembered that he was so muscular. His jeans and black T-shirt were well-fitted, and several others at the café had turned to look at him appreciatively.

"Sage," Trevor said, still smiling, "did you know I was coming before I even got here? I heard that you're the town psychic now." Trevor leaned down and put a hand up next to his mouth as if he were telling Sage a secret. In a stage whisper he said, "My father does not approve!"

Sage laughed. "Good! I've never wanted to impress a stuck-up snot like him. What brings you to town?"

Trevor's face sobered and he ran a hand self-consciously through his dark hair. "My dad, actually. He's sick. Cancer. My sister still lives here, but she's got a full-time job and three kids to deal with, so I came back to help out."

"Oh, I'm so sorry to hear that," Emily said, trying to take some of the attention away from Sage, whose cheeks had turned bright red. She always spoke honestly, and every now and then it really backfired. "I'm Emily. I was a couple of years ahead of you in school, I think."

Trevor nodded. "Yeah, you were with Sage in my brother's class, right?"

Oh, boy, another awkward subject. "Yeah."

There was a pause as Emily searched for something else to say. Trevor ran a hand through his hair again, making it stand up at strange angles.

"Are you looking for a job while you're here?" Sage asked. Emily relaxed, relieved that her friend had come up with something to keep the conversation going.

"I am, actually. I've been doing freelance graphic design for years. I don't think finding new clients in Oak Hill will be as easy as it was in Atlanta."

"Emily is looking for help." Sage looked at Emily pointedly.

"Oh! Yes, but it's just a part-time thing," Emily said quickly. "Two days a week, and sometimes on weekends if I'm having a big event and need extra help."

Trevor raised his eyebrows. "And what kind of work is it?"

"I own Eternal Rest Bed and Breakfast, out at the old cemetery. I just need someone to answer the phone and take care of any guests' needs twice a week so I can get out and run errands."

"And have a social life," interjected Sage.

"And have a social life," Emily echoed. "It might actually be perfect for you. When there are guests there during the week, it's usually not more than one or two couples at a time, and they're typically off doing things during the day.

So you'd just be sitting around most of the time, in case there was an emergency or if the guests came back early. You could bring your graphic design projects with you, if you wanted."

Trevor smiled. "I accept."

"You don't even know what my pay rate is!"

Trevor held up one finger. "First, it gets me out of my dad's house for a while. Second"—he raised another finger—"his medical bills are going to be astronomical. I'll take all the extra money I can get." He paused, then held up a third finger. "Plus, that place is haunted, right?"

Emily grinned. "I'll let you make up your own mind about that. Would you be available to come by tomorrow morning, maybe around nine? I can give you the rundown on everything. We're not booked tomorrow, so it will be nice and quiet."

Trevor readily agreed, then turned his attention back to Sage. He gently patted her hair. "I like this new you," he said approvingly. "Let's get together soon and catch up."

As soon as Trevor said his goodbye and headed inside the café, Sage turned to Emily with a satisfied look. "See, I told you that your short-staffed situation would soon be resolved."

"Yeah, but you didn't see it coming through any psychic channels. You literally saw him coming."

"Keen observation and trusting intuition are important, and not just for mediums." Sage sipped at her coffee happily.

Emily and Sage had been in the same class at school, and although they had known each other, they had never been friends. Sage had been awkward back then and always sat in the back of the classrooms, never really socializing with the other students. She would normally wear oversized hoodies, and she always carried her stack of books in her arms instead of using a backpack. It was like she was trying to build a shield between herself and the rest of the students.

"You and Trevor started hanging out after Dillan disappeared," Emily prompted.

Sage nodded. "I had always been a social outcast, and after his brother disappeared, Trevor's friends just dropped him. It was all too weird for them, and suddenly he wasn't a popular kid anymore. He wound up at my table during lunch one day, and I could sense that we were both feeling lonely and just sort of different from everyone else."

"Did you tell him you were psychic?"

"No. The only person I told back then was my grandma. She'd dropped enough hints about her own talents over the years that I knew she would understand."

"It must have been hard keeping big secrets from your family."

Sage barked a laugh. "If by 'big secrets,' you mean that I'm a lesbian, then no, it wasn't hard. My parents knew for years before I actually came out to them, and they've always been supportive. Telling them I was a psychic medium was a lot harder, and I thought my dad was going to hit the roof when I said I wanted to open up a practice here."

"Every family needs a good scandal." Emily popped the last bit of bagel into her mouth while she wiggled her eyebrows at Sage.

"What's yours going to be, I wonder?"

5

It had been a long time since Emily had felt spooked about being at Eternal Rest alone. At first, after Scott died, Emily had been grieving too much to think about the fact that she was sleeping alone in a haunted house, right next to a cemetery full of bodies and its own resident ghosts. By the time the veil of grief began to lift, Emily was simply used to the isolation. She had never been afraid of the spectral residents at Eternal Rest, anyway.

Tonight felt different. Maybe it was the lost-and-found emerald ring that made the house's atmosphere feel more ominous, but Emily found herself turning on more lights than normal and purposely scooting her kitchen chair around so that she faced the door while she ate dinner. She had an odd feeling, as if someone might walk through the open doorway without warning.

And maybe that was why Emily's thoughts instantly went to paranormal activity when she walked into her bedroom later and found one of her grandmother's gold hoop earrings lying on top of the jewelry box instead of inside it. As soon as she noticed the earring, Emily looked around the room, almost expecting to see someone there.

Emily gave her head a little shake. She had rummaged through the crowded jewelry box earlier, looking for the carved wooden bangle bracelet she usually wore with her yellow sweater. She had probably left the earring on top of the box by accident, too busy to realize that not all of the jewelry she'd taken out during her search for the bracelet had made it safely back inside.

Now, Emily did put the gold hoop away, deliberately noting that she put it next to its mate in the back left corner. If it moved again, she would definitely notice.

I need a bath, Emily thought. *A nice, hot, relaxing bath. I've earned it.*

No sooner had Emily turned on the tap of the clawfoot tub, though, than she heard a faint knock over the noise of the water. She hastily twisted the old iron handles to stop the water and listened carefully. Just silence. Emily chided herself and reached for the handles again.

This time, there was definitely a knocking sound, but Emily instantly knew it was nothing paranormal. It was simply someone at the front door. That was perhaps stranger than a ghostly explanation, since she got few uninvited visitors, especially after dinnertime.

Emily gave the tub a longing glance, then headed down the hall to the front door. "Who is it?" she called, her hand poised on the lock.

"Benjamin Williams." Not Ben. Not Benny. Benjamin. Trevor, Dillan, and their sister must have had a tough time growing up with Mr. Williams's strict, no-nonsense parenting style. Of course, most people thought that was why Dillan had just disappeared at the beginning of their senior year. He'd simply had enough and left. Some gossips speculated that Dillan's fate had been much more sinister, and that someday his dead body would be found in the woods around Oak Hill.

Emily liked to think he had escaped to a great new life somewhere. She preferred her dead bodies buried in the ground in a cemetery, and she liked the idea of happy endings.

Opening the door cautiously, Emily found herself face-to-face with the formidable Mr. Williams, except he wasn't really all that formidable anymore. He was thin, and his arm shook slightly as he extended a hand to Emily.

"We've met once or twice around town," he began. "I'm Benjamin Williams."

"Yes, sir." Emily suddenly felt like a teenager again, even though she had only met him once back then, when he had spoken at their school for career day. She had met him again later as an adult, when he attended her grandpa's funeral. "This is a surprise! Come in."

Mr. Williams walked in slowly, and although his back was now slightly rounded, it was easy to see he had once been a tall, well-built man. Like Trevor, Emily thought. Dillan's physique had been similar, matching his role as a star football player for the Oak Hill Devils before his disappearance.

Emily ushered Mr. Williams into the parlor, pointing him to the sofa. "Would you like some tea? I have iced tea, but I can make it hot, too."

Mr. Williams declined, so she sat primly on the edge of a wingback chair, her back ramrod straight. Dillan had often talked about how hard their dad was on him and his siblings, and the kids at Oak Hill High School had viewed him as the hometown tyrant.

Once she was an adult, Emily had realized that Mr. Williams was actually well-respected by the community in Oak Hill. He had inherited the family construction business, and he was known for doing quality work with fair prices. Her own grandparents had even used his company while converting and restoring the house.

"I'm sure you're wondering why I'm here," he began after gingerly sitting on the sofa. Emily simply nodded. "Well, Trevor told me he's coming out here to do some work for you. I wanted to come and say thank you."

"Oh, Mr. Williams, there's no need to thank me. I've been in desperate need of an assistant, and running into Trevor today was really lucky."

Mr. Williams held up a hand, clearly not finished yet. "I realize it's a win-win situation, but you hired Trevor on the spot. It's only his third day back in Oak Hill, and he's already got work. He's doing it for me, you know. I'm sick." Mr. Williams gestured to himself.

"I was very sorry to hear the news."

"Yes, well, first my wife and now me. I'll be with her again by the end of the year. But, in the meantime, I'm collecting medical bills like my wife collected those little stuffed animals that used to be all the rage. Binky Babies, or whatever they were called. Anyway, I know Trevor only took the work because he wants to help me pay those off. So, whether you were aware of it or not, you really did me a big favor by hiring him."

Emily could feel herself blushing self-consciously, and she averted her gaze to the carpet. "I'm glad I could help," she said softly.

"You had your own loss a couple years ago."

Emily looked up and saw sympathy in Mr. Williams's gaze. "Yes, my husband died in a car crash on the way back from visiting his mom in Alabama."

Mr. Williams nodded slowly. "It's not easy letting our loved ones go. I miss Maria every day. At least I had forty years with her. You weren't so lucky. My condolences, dear."

"Thank you, Mr. Williams," Emily said with feeling. She hadn't expected such kind sympathy from him. So many people had offered their condolences in the past two years that the repeated phrases and words of comfort had started to lose their meaning. This time, though, Emily could feel the sincerity.

She sighed. "It's lonely sometimes, but my guests keep

my life interesting." Struck with a wave of affection for the man, she continued, "You know, Mr. Williams, if you ever want to come with Trevor when he's working, you're more than welcome. You can make yourself at home here in the parlor, or out on the porch if it's a nice day. There are always drinks and snacks in the kitchen."

"That's kind of you. I might just do that." Mr. Williams smiled and rose. "Well, I'm off. I told Trevor I was going to the grocery store for some beer—I'm not supposed to drink alcohol while I'm doing chemo, but what's the point of living if you can't have a few drinks, right? He'll get worried if I'm not back soon. I knew he'd object to me coming out here to see you. He'd think it was unnecessary."

"Maybe it wasn't necessary, but it is very much appreciated. I hope to see you again soon." Emily was surprised to realize she meant it.

Emily stayed on the porch until the taillights of Mr. Williams's car had disappeared around the curve in the road. Even though he had brought up Scott's death, the unexpected visit had actually helped lift her spirits. Feeling lighter than she had all evening, Emily went back inside, locked the door, and decided that only an emergency would keep her from getting into the bathtub this time.

Trevor arrived exactly ten minutes early on Tuesday morning. It was drizzling, and the sky was covered with gray clouds. Emily figured she was the only bed and breakfast owner who loved welcoming newcomers to her home on days like this. The gloomy pall gave a spooky vibe to the house, making even the bright white gingerbread trim along the top of the porch seem subdued.

"I've been in the cemetery, but not the house. Wow, this

is impressive. You've done a great job with it." Trevor's praise seemed sincere. He was craning his neck up to admire the crown molding along the edge of the ceiling in the parlor.

"Let me guess: you used to go to the cemetery not to appreciate the historic monuments, but to drink beer in a place where no adults would catch you."

Trevor gave Emily a lopsided smile. "Who didn't?"

"Me! My grandparents lived here, and they hated having to chase teenagers out all the time."

"How often do you chase kids out of there? And please tell me that you shout 'get off my lawn' when you do it!"

Emily frowned teasingly. "I'm not old enough for that yet. Besides, most of the high school kids sneak in their beers at… I don't actually know where they go these days. It's not here, though. I've only had a handful of after-hours trespassers."

"Good. That means kicking people off the property will probably not be one of my duties."

"It's doubtful, especially during the day. Come on, I'll give you the full tour and the basics for answering the phone. I'll also give you some tips for how to answer the more unusual questions."

"Such as?"

"Such as whether or not a guest can bring along a dog that can allegedly see ghosts. The answer is no."

"Duly noted."

There wasn't really all that much information for Emily to impart, and Trevor picked up all of it quickly, including some of the basic facts about the history of the house and the cemetery. They were at the top of the stairs on the second floor when there was a loud rumble and a low grating sound from downstairs. Emily could feel a slight vibration in the boards beneath her feet.

Emily raced down the stairs, heading for the source of

the sound, as Trevor followed more cautiously. The noises had seemed to come from the kitchen. When she got in there, the table had been pushed from its normal spot in the corner to directly in front of the countertop. It had moved several feet, leaving long scrape marks in the wooden floor where the legs had traveled. Everything on the kitchen counter had moved, too, and the microwave was now teetering right on the edge.

"Oh," Emily said, too surprised to get anything else out.

"It wasn't like that when we were in here a few minutes ago," Trevor noted, hovering in the doorway. His eyes were wide.

"You wanted haunted." Emily could hear the surprise and slight nervousness in her own voice. A ring moving was one thing, but now a piece of furniture? Pushing the table like that must have taken a massive amount of energy on the part of whatever paranormal entity had done it. And there was zero doubt in Emily's mind that it had been a ghost.

Trevor's voice was quiet when he spoke next. "So, what do we do now? Are we supposed to talk to it?"

Emily shrugged. "Actually, I'm not sure what to do. This is Sage's territory. I could ask a ghost fifty questions, but I'm not a medium, so I'd never hear their answer. Can you help me slide the table back into place? At least the table will cover some of the marks on the floor." Already, Emily was wondering how much it would cost to get the kitchen floor sanded and refinished. *Too much,* she told herself. *The guests don't come in here, so the floor can just stay that way.*

A short while later, Trevor continued to look uncomfortable as he signed the contract Emily had printed out, and she was worried he might back out of the job offer. "Something like that has never happened before," she assured him, sounding almost apologetic. "Unless Sage is here conducting a séance, the activity is usually limited to things like sounds or cold spots. Mrs. Thompson, our newest ghost, sometimes moves suitcases or does other little things to help guests. You'll hear someone walking upstairs from time to time, but it's not really that scary if it happens in broad daylight. You learn to kind of get used to it. I try to think of it as if they're really good roommates. You hear them once in a while, but they never leave dirty dishes in the sink and they mostly keep to themselves."

Trevor took a deep breath. "What happened today definitely caught me off guard, but don't worry. I'm not going to run out of here screaming just because a ghost wants to rearrange the furniture."

Promising to be back at nine again on Thursday for his first day of work, Trevor left. As soon as he was gone, Emily marched into the kitchen and began to inspect the room. Luckily, the microwave and the porcelain dishes stacked next to the sink hadn't moved far enough to actually fall to the floor. Emily put the dishes in the dishwasher just in case the ghost moved things on the countertop again.

After double-checking that everything was back in its proper place, Emily stepped back and said loudly, "If you're trying to tell me something, you're not doing a good job of it."

Nothing happened for the rest of the day. Emily went to bed Tuesday night feeling assured that, like the ring, the moving table and kitchen items had been some kind of weird, isolated incident. If Rhonda and Tim really did have some kind of entity or energy attached to them, it was possible they had left a little bit behind, and it expended itself by rearranging the kitchen. Emily considered calling Sage to ask her about it, but she didn't want to risk having her theory disproven. She much preferred to stick with the idea that whatever had caused all of these items to move had done its thing and was now long gone.

When Emily woke up the next morning, though, it was clear the entity was not only still there, but it was getting stronger.

6

Every single item in Emily's room had been moved. Not by much, but enough that Emily instantly noticed the changes. The dresser, vanity, and nightstand had all shifted a few inches away from the walls they ordinarily stood against. The lamp on the nightstand, which normally arched toward the bed, had been turned to face the other direction. Emily's jewelry box was now sitting directly in the middle of the dresser instead of in its usual perch on the right side. Even the photos hanging on the walls were crooked, all perfectly tilted to the same angle. Suddenly, the photos of Scott smiling happily looked slightly sinister.

Emily slid out of bed slowly. The room seemed different, not just because of everything being slightly out of place. The atmosphere had changed. It felt stuffy, and the air had a stillness to it that made her think of the third-floor attic room when she didn't air it out for a long time.

She turned, taking in every detail of her bedroom. All of the familiar things were still there, but they were all so uncomfortably strange now. Her eyes landed on the bed, and even it had been moved. It was no longer centered under the wedding photo that hung above it.

Emily felt goosebumps raise on her arms. Something had done all of this while she soundly slept. It had either been done silently or that same something had ensured she didn't wake up while her entire room was thrown into disarray.

Fearing what she might find, Emily opened her bedroom door and peered down the hallway. The paintings hung along the walls were still neatly level. She stepped into the kitchen, but everything was in order there, too. A quick check of the rest of the house revealed that everything outside her bedroom was untouched. Whichever one of Eternal Rest's ghosts was causing this, they must be doing it to get her attention.

Knowing that Sage tended to stay up late at night and get out of bed later than most people, Emily didn't want to call her too early. Instead, she spent an anxious hour sitting at the kitchen table, barely touching her breakfast or her coffee as she wondered what could be so serious that a ghost would go to so much trouble. It took energy for ghosts to manifest any kind of paranormal activity, with moving objects and making themselves visible considered to be the things that required the most effort. It must have taken an extraordinary amount of energy for a ghost to manipulate every single object in Emily's room, including a bed that even she, a living person, couldn't move alone.

Maybe it was a concerted effort, Emily thought. Maybe all of the ghosts had gotten together to get her attention. But for what?

The hands on the wall clock had just slid into the eight o'clock position and Emily had just picked up her cell phone when it rang. It was Sage's name on the screen, and Emily answered with a surprised hello.

"I had a dream that you were in distress. Tell me what's going on." Sage did not waste time on small talk when she was "chasing ghosts," as Emily liked to call it.

Emily breathlessly filled her in, trying to express concern without sounding too scared. "I think someone is trying to tell me something," she concluded.

"Gee, you think?" Sage had stayed mostly silent while Emily related her experience, and Emily was surprised to hear sarcasm in her tone now. When Sage spoke again, though, she could hear the concern, too. "I think the important thing here is that you weren't harmed. Keep that in mind when, not if, something else happens. Clearly, the ghost—whomever it is—isn't trying to hurt you. You're right, this seems like a way of getting attention. You want me to do a séance? I can come over once I close the shop tonight."

"I have guests coming in this afternoon, and they're staying through Sunday. I'd rather not kick off their visit with a surprise séance." While many people opted for the Spirited Saturday Night weekends, plenty of other guests simply wanted a relaxing stay in a charming, albeit haunted, Victorian home. Having a chance encounter with a ghost was one thing; actively looking for one was another. Emily ran her free hand through her hair. "What should I do?"

"Ask it what it wants. Not just once, but often. Your message is more likely to be heard if it's repeated. Also, stop to listen for an answer."

"But I can't hear ghosts."

"Not the way I do, certainly," Sage replied, "but you've heard the knocking, the footsteps. You've smelled things and have sensed cold spots and shifts in a room's energy. So just listen. It might not be a voice you hear, but you might glean other information that can lead you to an answer."

Sage hesitated a moment before she continued. "Again, I don't think you're in any danger, but I'm glad you're not going to be there alone tonight. Call me the second anything else happens."

"I will." Emily hung up the phone feeling slightly reassured, but still she dreaded going back into her bedroom.

Instead, she gazed across the kitchen. "If you can hear me, please tell me what you want me to know."

Nothing. The house was completely silent.

Steeling herself, Emily went back into the bedroom. This time, now that she knew what to expect, the sight wasn't so jarring, but the same heavy atmosphere still pervaded the space. She set about putting everything back into its proper spot, taking note of anything else that might be out of place or missing, but even her grandmother's earrings were still nested inside the jewelry box.

The bed would take two people to move, so Emily would have to wait until Trevor came out the next day. Moving her bedroom furniture was probably not the first task he was expecting for his new job.

Emily continued calling out to the ghost who had visited her room, pausing to listen every now and then as she showered and got ready for the day. She was answered each time by the same silence.

By the time she was dressed in jeans and a sweater, Emily had already decided to get out of the house for a while. She called the bakery and let the owner, Trish, know that she would pick up her order in person that day. If she hurried, she could go to the bank and pick up a few things at the grocery store before coming back to await her guests' arrival.

The sense of urgency to get her errands run in time helped Emily focus on something other than her ghosts. The rain of the day before had ushered in a late-season cold front, and the wind made Emily's nose feel icy on the short walk to the car.

Two hours later, Emily was so busy congratulating herself on getting her to-do list accomplished that she wasn't thinking at all of her ghosts as she came home and unlocked the front door. She dropped the bakery order on the kitchen counter, put away all of the groceries, and sat down at the kitchen table to eat the sandwich she had bought while she was in town.

It was the sound of something falling that brought her mind back to ghosts.

The noise came from her bedroom, and when Emily hurried in, she saw her jewelry box dumped onto the floor in front of the dresser. One corner of the wooden box had chipped off when it hit the floor, and several earrings had skittered halfway across the room. This time, when Emily addressed the ghost, she sounded more like an angry parent. "I don't know what you're trying to say," she lectured. "You can't expect me to understand if you're just moving all of my things. Focus, and try something else! Try to send a clear message. Also, you broke my jewelry box! That is not cool!"

Emily was still in a bad mood when her guests, an engaged couple in their mid-twenties named Brianne and Nathan, arrived. Nathan was tall and skinny, with shaggy brown hair and an outfit that looked like it had come from an outdoors store. Brianne looked less ready for adventure in yoga pants and an oversized sweatshirt that kept slipping off one shoulder. Emily smiled at them and hoped they wouldn't see through the facade. Apparently, they didn't: Nathan kept pretending he was already seeing ghosts, and Brianne kept giggling about it.

"There's one in the corner! Look at his hideous face!" Nathan said, simultaneously grabbing Brianne around the waist. She squealed, then giggled again, the blonde bun plopped on top of her head bouncing in time with her excited movements.

"Our ghosts are very good-looking, you know," Emily chided. Normally, she would have been amused by Nathan's enthusiasm, but in her mood, it was just annoying. She was putting the couple in the guest room above the dining room, as far from her own room as possible. The other rooms would be filled on Friday.

"Have you seen them?" Brianne's eyes were wide.

"I haven't, but I knew one of them when she was alive. A nice elderly woman named Mrs. Thompson who definitely doesn't have a hideous face."

"Mrs. Thompson," said Brianne dreamily. "Did the love of her life die here, and she comes back looking for him in the afterlife?"

Emily actually laughed at that vision of her friend and former employee. "No, she just loved working here so much that she hasn't left yet. Although, I do like the lost love idea; it sounds much more romantic. Come on, I'll show you up to your room. Breakfast will be ready beginning at seven each morning, and just let me know if you need anything or if you want recommendations on things to do around town."

"Our schedule is pretty full already," admitted Nathan. "You have the only haunted bed and breakfast in this part of the state, but there are a lot of haunted spots to visit during the day."

Emily nodded knowingly. "Of course, the North Georgia Ghosts itinerary. That book has brought me a lot of business. Oh, but if the burger place in downtown Oak Hill is on your list, you can skip it. That story was debunked, unfortunately."

"Were they faking all the strange noises?"

"Rats inside the walls. So you probably don't want to eat there, either."

Emily kept a close watch on the house for the rest of the day, often pausing to simply listen. Brianne and Nathan went out to explore a few haunted places and have dinner in town, so Emily had the house to herself again until she heard them come in at ten o'clock that night. Once their footsteps had retreated upstairs, Emily locked up the front door, double-checked the back door, and went to bed.

It wasn't noises from upstairs that woke Emily this time. Instead, it was a nightmare that left Emily gasping. She found herself wide awake and sitting up in bed, one hand held against her neck.

In the dream, she had felt strong hands around her neck, cutting off her airway. She glanced down and saw arms that were too skinny and suntanned to be her own, the hands reaching up to claw at the attacker's. She could hear him breathing heavily behind her, but all she could see was darkness ahead. As she strained to turn her head in an effort to loosen the grip around her neck, a bright yellow pinpoint of light came into view briefly. Then, with the desperate, resigned thought that she was dying, she closed her eyes.

Emily woke up right as she felt the life ebbing from her, her hands automatically reaching up to touch her neck. She quickly turned on the nightstand lamp and looked around, but she was alone. The dream had felt so real, and her breathing was so strained she almost expected to see someone standing there, waiting to strangle her again. Emily stared down at her own arms. She slowly flexed her fingers, comforted by being in her own body again.

Finally, when both her breathing and her heartbeat had slowed down, Emily said to the empty room, "If that was you, I got the message. You were strangled to death by someone. This is a good start."

Being killed in a dream was definitely not Emily's preferred method of spirit communication, but she did, at least, have something more concrete than simply a ghost who liked to rearrange furniture and play with jewelry.

Had one of her resident ghosts been murdered? And if

so, why was that ghost just now trying to send a message about it? Emily felt certain it was a woman, and judging by the hands around her neck and the bulk of the body behind her, it had been a man who murdered her. She had nothing else to go on. Where it had happened, how long ago it had happened and, most importantly, the identity of the people involved were still unknown.

Part of Emily argued that it was just a dream, but her instincts told her it was more than that. And Sage had told her to listen to her instincts. Sage had also said to call her the moment anything paranormal happened, but Emily wasn't going to bother anyone at—she glanced at her alarm clock—almost three o'clock in the morning.

Instead, Emily put on a bathrobe and went into the parlor with a book. She felt like she needed to not only get up and move around a little to shake off the dream, but also to get out of her room for a while.

Emily had only been reading for a few minutes when she heard a muffled shriek from upstairs. She tensed, but the only other sound she heard was the squeaking of the floorboards. *Maybe I'm not the only one having nightmares.*

Around four, Emily finally felt her eyelids drooping, and she went back to bed. This time, nothing disturbed her sleep, with the exception of the alarm clock.

Brianne and Nathan were not the early risers that Rhonda and Tim had been. Emily was on her second cup of coffee when she finally heard them come downstairs. She had already arranged breakfast on the dining room table, so she stayed in the kitchen. Normally, guests would simply help themselves to the food, and Emily was surprised when Nathan appeared in the doorway.

"Uh, ma'am?" he said hesitantly.

"Emily," she answered. She was too young for someone that old to call her *ma'am*.

"I have a weird question." Nathan shifted from one foot to the other as he glanced quickly down the hallway.

"Come in. Do you want to sit?" Emily gestured to a chair at the table.

Nathan hesitated, then nodded. He pushed the chair closer to Emily's, sat down, and leaned in, his voice barely above a whisper. "Do people ever have weird dreams here?"

Emily felt her stomach lurch. Taking a guess, she asked, "Were you being choked to death?"

Nathan's eyes widened, and he sat back. "Yes. Well, no, not me, but Brianne. She had the dream. It really upset her, and I told her it was just a dream, but…"

"But it felt like something more," Emily finished for him. "I had the same dream last night. Let's go talk to Brianne."

They found Brianne sitting at the dining room table. She had a croissant and a steaming cup of coffee sitting in front of her, but she sat perfectly still, staring at the wall with a glazed expression.

Emily sat down next to her and spoke softly. "Tell me about the dream."

Brianne blinked and turned to Emily with a start. "Oh, good morning. I didn't hear you come in. Nathan told you I had a nightmare."

"Yes."

"It wasn't just a dream."

"That does seem to be the theme of the day. You tell me about yours, and then I'll tell you about mine."

Haltingly, Brianne related a dream that was the same as Emily's: She was in a dark place, and two hands were clamped around her neck. She had also woken up straining for air. "At first, I didn't even realize I was in someone else's body," Brianne said, "but there were a bunch of friendship bracelets around my wrist, and I haven't worn those in years. I've had plenty of nightmares, but nothing has ever felt so real."

"I had the same dream," Emily said sympathetically. "We—my friend Sage and I—believe a ghost is trying to communicate. It started a few days ago. One of my guests had a ring go missing, and later it just appeared in the middle of her bed. Actually, she had a dream, too, but in hers, a man just ripped off her necklace and she felt pain at her neck. There was no dying in her dream."

Everyone sat in silence for a few moments. Emily was busy worrying that these guests were going to want to leave, and she was weighing whether or not to offer them a full refund right then and there. Nathan was still standing, and he began to pace back and forth between the door and the sideboard.

It was Brianne who spoke first. "Count us in."

"Really?" Nathan's tone was hopeful.

"In for what?" Emily asked skeptically.

Brianne nodded firmly. "That dream was scary as hell, but if there's some ghost trying to tell us that she was murdered, then I want to help her. That's the only reason she'd give us a dream like this, right? Because she needs help finding out who did this to her." Her mind made up, Brianne began eating as if the dream had left her starving.

"Not necessarily," Emily said slowly. "Traumatic moments are sometimes repeated in the afterlife, and often it's the moment of death. Events like violent murders"— she paused, searching for the right words—"they sort of imprint themselves, like paranormal energy that lingers in a place. So what we're seeing could be something like that: leftover energy from a traumatic event."

"Does this happen to you and your guests often?" Nathan asked.

"Nooo," Emily conceded. "This is completely new. It's like it just came out of nowhere."

Now Nathan was smiling. "So it's not just leftover energy. We're going to help a ghost! This is going to be such a cool vacation."

While Emily certainly appreciated that her guests weren't already packing up to leave, she did want to curb their enthusiasm a little bit. Before she accepted any kind of help or took any further steps to try to communicate with this ghost, she needed Sage's input. Emily still felt that Sage's earlier opinion of the ghost not wanting to harm anyone was true, but after the vivid nightmare, she also didn't want to invite any paranormal activity that might feel even more realistic. Unconsciously, Emily raised her hand to her neck and rubbed the skin lightly.

"Sage is a psychic medium, and she conducts all of our séances here, so I'm going to get her advice," Emily said. "If you're up for it, which I suspect you are, then maybe she can come out and we can try to communicate with the ghost. We're going to have a full house beginning tomorrow, so the sooner we can try to help this ghost, the better. However"—she held up a hand as Nathan and Brianne looked at her excitedly—"I want to wait until I've talked to her before we do anything else. You wouldn't believe how much the paranormal activity in this house has increased in the past few days. I don't want us to get in over our heads. You two stick with your North Georgia Ghosts itinerary, and Sage and I will work on a plan for tonight."

Nathan's eyes narrowed. "Will you be safe here by yourself?"

As if in answer, the sound of the handle rattling in the front door echoed down the hall, followed by the chime of the doorbell. "My assistant just arrived." Emily glanced at her watch. "A few minutes early, no less."

Trevor was bouncing on the balls of his feet when Emily opened the door. He beamed at her. "I'm ready for my first…" His voice trailed off when he saw her strained expression.

"It's okay. There has been some more redecorating by

this ghost, and now some horrible dreams of being murdered. Come in." Emily tried to brighten her tone at that last part, but the fake cheer sounded ridiculous in her ears.

Brianne and Nathan were in the hallway as Trevor came inside, and they quickly introduced themselves. "We're going to help with your ghost problem," Nathan announced grandly.

Trevor turned slightly and raised an eyebrow in Emily's direction. "I'll fill you in," she promised. "In the meantime, want some breakfast?"

"Already the best job ever," Trevor answered, following Emily into the dining room. Brianne and Nathan hadn't eaten much, and Emily decided a second breakfast wouldn't do any harm. Besides, she hated to let the food go to waste.

As they ate, Emily explained everything that had happened since Trevor left Eternal Rest on Tuesday. He looked concerned but certainly not scared.

Nathan came in as they spoke, a camera in one hand and a tape recorder in the other. "We're going to practice our ghost-hunting skills today, so we'll be ready for tonight!"

"Great!" Emily said, trying to match Nathan's perkiness.

As soon as they left, she chuckled. "They are very… enthusiastic about this paranormal activity. I wish I could feel the same."

Trevor drained his coffee cup and looked earnestly at Emily. "So, what now?"

"I'm going to run up and neaten their room, then throw these dishes into the dishwasher. I don't actually need to go into town today since I got my errands run yesterday, but I'm happy to have your company here, considering the situation. I'll run to the bakery later to get the things for tomorrow's breakfast so I can save Trish from having to stop by here this afternoon. That's kind of it. I hope you brought some work with you."

Trevor nodded. "My laptop bag is in my car. I'll go grab it and set up in here."

"That reminds me," said Emily, rising and heading for the parlor. "I'm going to give you a key to the front door so you can just let yourself in from now on."

As Trevor went to his car, Emily went upstairs to make sure her guests had a nice, neat room waiting for them when they got back from exploring. Both that and the dishes were quickly done, so Emily gave Trevor the run of the house and walked to the cemetery. The sun was shining again, and making a lap of each ring path was Emily's favorite kind of exercise. Trevor promised he was willing to brave any potential paranormal activity that might happen during Emily's short absence.

Emily called Sage as she made a beeline for the top of the hill. Starting at the very top and working her way down around each ring path always seemed less strenuous, and mentally it gave her a relaxing "winding down" feeling.

Sage agreed with Emily's assertion that the dreams were ominous but not dangerous, and she agreed to come to Eternal Rest for a late-night séance, just as soon as she and her wife finished dinner. "Jen is making enchiladas," Sage explained. "No way am I missing that!"

Emily felt better knowing Sage would be helping them find some answers that night, which hopefully meant no one would be plagued by nightmares. If the ghost could simply communicate with Sage, then there would be no need for the dreams. Of course, Emily reminded herself, with ghosts it was rarely that easy.

As soon as Emily reached the top of the hill, she spotted Reed and his team at work on the Clements plot. She was nearly hidden from their view between the high granite walls of two mausoleums, so she waited until she was on the next path down the hill before waving at them.

The three people on the restoration team smiled and returned the greeting, but Reed only nodded curtly. Frowning, Emily took a shortcut to him, cutting down a narrow brick path that connected the second and third ring paths.

"Did you have a nightmare, too?" Emily asked. It sounded stupid and incredibly unlikely, but it was the first thought in her mind.

"No, but I am trying to solve a mystery." Reed gently took Emily by the elbow and steered her away from the plot so they could speak privately. "You haven't been using any of the tools we keep in the barn, have you?"

The barn sat behind Eternal Rest, and ever since Emily could remember, the little one-story brick building had been the place to stash the city's collection of lawn-care equipment and tools. A workshop had been set up on one side for headstones that needed extra restoration attention.

Emily shook her head.

"I didn't think so, but we locked them up in there on Friday afternoon, after we finished our work for the week. When we got here on Monday, several of them were missing. I was going to ask you about them, but when we brought the rest of our equipment out here, we found the tools. They were in a pile right next to this plot. There is no way we overlooked them when we packed up on Friday. I thought maybe you had borrowed them, then forgotten you'd taken them from the barn instead of the work site."

Emily absentmindedly brought one hand up to her ponytail and began winding a lock of hair around her index finger. She knew Reed believed in ghosts, but she didn't want to concern him. Slowly, she said, "Do you think it could have been paranormal?"

Reed's eyes narrowed. "Why in the world would your mind jump right to that?"

"We've had some strange activity at the house. It started Sunday night. Plus, don't forget that some ghost hunters recently dug up that century-old story about a traveling salesman who was sleeping in the barn one night, but wound up being found dead in the cemetery. I've never had reason to think the barn is haunted, but the paranormal activity happening in the house is unprecedented, too, so maybe things are getting stirred up all over the property."

Reed pursed his lips and looked thoughtfully at the Clements plot. "I suppose it could be paranormal."

"Are you free tonight? Sage is coming over to host a séance, and it will just be me and her, plus our two guests. You're welcome to join us. In fact, I'd really appreciate it if you did. If it wasn't someone simply forgetting your tools out here, then it could be a part of whatever is going on in the house, and you being there tonight might help us get answers. I'll even make dinner beforehand, and I'll fill you in on everything while we eat."

"I'm getting used to you feeding me every time I come over there, you know." Reed gave Emily a lopsided smile. "Yeah, I'll come. I've never done one of these séances you two put on, and I don't know if I'm entirely comfortable with it, but"—Reed shrugged—"since dinner is involved…"

Emily shoved his arm playfully. "Sage is coming around nine, so eight for dinner."

"As long as I get to scold any ghosts who borrowed my tools without asking."

"Thanks, Reed. See you tonight, then." Emily turned and continued her walk, wondering why the ghost was covering so much territory. If it was trying to send a message, what did moving tools communicate? Of course,

Emily reminded herself, the tools might just be a case of someone forgetting to put things where they belong. There was no reason to jump to any paranormal conclusion.

"Skepticism is the greatest tool a ghost hunter has," Emily said softly to herself. Teams of paranormal investigators stayed at Eternal Rest regularly, and Emily happily let them stay up into the wee hours to look for evidence of her ghosts. Some groups would even set up their equipment in the cemetery, but Emily always insisted on accompanying them to keep an eye on things. The last thing she wanted was for someone to accidentally damage one of the monuments or take a wrong step in the dark. It was during a hot, sticky night last August when Emily had been miserably swatting at mosquitoes while overseeing a group's work in the cemetery that she overheard one of them say those words. They had stuck with her ever since, and she often repeated the phrase to herself when she heard the upstairs floorboards creaking, even when there were no guests staying at Eternal Rest.

Emily finished her lap of the lowest ring path and moved onto the path that led out of the cemetery. The brick wall that surrounded the property was only three feet high, hardly enough to keep anyone out, but that hadn't stopped the builders from adding an ornate iron gate with wrought-iron magnolia blossoms that arched over it. This main entrance split into two paths outside the cemetery: a narrow dirt trail through the grass that led to the house and a wider brick lane that matched the paths inside the cemetery. That one led straight to the road, and for nearly a century, hearses—horse-drawn at first, and later motorized—had carried bodies into the cemetery and up the hill to their final resting place. Now, it just led visitors from a small, grassy roadside parking area to the front gate.

It was the narrow dirt path that Emily walked now, and when she looked ahead, she realized Trevor was sitting on the front porch swing. As long as he had taken the cordless phone out there with him in case anyone called about making reservations, Emily didn't care where he sat. In fact, as nice as it was outside, she figured he had the best seat in the house.

It wasn't until she was walking up the front steps that Emily could see how stiffly Trevor was sitting. His chest heaved, and his mouth hung open as he drew in big gasps of air. He was holding his right hand in his left, and as Emily watched, a drop of blood escaped his grip and splattered to the porch floor.

8

"Trevor? Oh, no, are you okay? What happened?" Emily flew up the final steps and kneeled down in front of Trevor.

His eyes glanced her way, but he was wildly looking all around him, as if he expected an attack from any side. Emily put a firm hand on his arm. "Trevor!"

This time, his eyes met hers and held. "Deep breaths," Emily said.

Trevor took a shaky breath, then blew it out with a huff. He closed his eyes, shook his head slightly, then looked at Emily again. "I'm okay," he said, his voice quiet but even.

"You're bleeding."

Trevor glanced down at his hand. "Oh, no, I'm getting blood on your porch. I'm so sorry."

"It's fine. I've got a first-aid kit stashed in the closet under the base of the stairs. I'm going to go get it, and I'll be right back."

"Just be careful."

"Of what?"

"Of whatever did this to me."

Emily swallowed hard. She didn't like the idea that a ghost had hurt Trevor, but she didn't feel any surprise at his words. She didn't think any ordinary accident would have caused Trevor to react so strongly.

The front door was standing wide open, and as soon as Emily stepped over the threshold, she felt the same heaviness that had pervaded her bedroom after her furniture had been rearranged. There was an odd, acrid smell floating in the air, too. The dining room and parlor doors were both open, as they usually were when the rooms weren't being used for an event, and Emily glanced quickly through both doorways as she advanced. Nothing looked out of place in either of them. That was a relief.

The closet was tucked into a small space under the bottom stairs, and Emily snatched the first-aid kit out of it, resisting the urge to go check on her bedroom and the kitchen. There would be time for that after she helped Trevor.

Back on the porch, Emily knelt down in front of Trevor and quickly opened the kit. She paused to take her own advice, inhaling a deep breath and letting it out slowly. She had gotten her first-aid certification when she took over Eternal Rest, but the most she had ever had to do for a guest was to fill an ice pack when someone sprained an ankle. Emily fished out a square of gauze and pulled on a pair of plastic gloves.

Emily gingerly took Trevor's right hand and turned it over. There was a gash across his palm, but it wasn't bleeding as badly as Emily had feared. She pressed the gauze against it as Trevor winced. As she kept pressure applied to slow the bleeding, she said gently, "Tell me what happened."

"It was weird, Emily. I was sitting there at the dining room table with my laptop, and there was this noise from the back of the house like someone had run a semi into the wall. I ran back there, but I couldn't tell if the sound came from your room or the kitchen. I checked in the kitchen, and everything looked fine. I tried your door, but it was locked. The noise was so loud and so unexpected that my adrenaline had kicked in, and I just stood there in the hall for a minute, trying to calm down.

"And then I heard the noise again, directly behind me, in the kitchen. I turned around, but everything still looked fine. I walked in, thinking maybe something inside one of the cabinets had fallen. I started looking through them, and your microwave just suddenly exploded."

Emily stared up at Trevor, unconsciously gripping his injured hand so hard he said, "Ow!"

"Sorry," Emily said, loosening her fingers. "My microwave… exploded?"

"Yeah. It was like one of those videos online, where someone sticks a bunch of silverware in a microwave and then turns it on. There was a bright, flickering light inside your microwave, and as soon as I looked down and saw it, it just blew up. The front door flew open and there was this wave of… I don't even know what to call it. It wasn't heat. More like a rushing wind, but I'm talking hurricane force. It knocked me backwards, and I went sprawling. I got up and ran out here. I had just sat down when you came up."

Now it was Emily's turn to panic, and she recognized that what she had smelled inside the house was burning electrical components. "Is my kitchen on fire?"

Trevor's face registered surprise, but it was from concern rather than shock that Emily was thinking of her kitchen's welfare instead of his. "Oh, I hadn't even thought of that. I hope not."

"I'm going to check." Emily dashed back inside the house, her mind struggling to process this new information. Had Trevor been attacked by a ghost, or had the ghost accidentally hurt him in its effort to communicate?

There was no smoke coming from the kitchen when I went inside the house before, Emily told herself, trying to curb her racing mind. *There wasn't then, and there's still not, and it's going to be okay.*

Thankfully, it was okay. The microwave was sitting in its normal spot, but like Trevor had said, the door had been forced open, and it was misshapen, like something inside the microwave had been pushing against the door so hard it had warped.

Quickly, Emily unplugged the microwave and tapped its side with a finger. It wasn't hot, but just to be on the safe side, she swiftly slid the pile of junk mail and other little items that had accumulated on top of it onto the counter, grabbed the microwave, and marched with it out to the front porch. She continued down the steps and placed it right in the middle of the driveway. Since the driveway was concrete, she figured that if any kind of electrical fire had been festering inside the microwave, it would burn itself out without catching anything else on fire. The entire appliance felt cool to the touch, though, so Emily doubted that would happen. Still, she was definitely going to have to buy a new microwave. *After we take care of this ghost.*

Slowly, looking over her shoulder every few seconds to see if the microwave was doing anything *weird*—as Trevor put it—Emily climbed back up the steps. She looked down at her hands and realized she was still wearing the protective gloves. She stripped them off carefully, turning them inside out as she did so, and dropped them unceremoniously on the floor.

"My kitchen is not on fire," Emily finally said.

"I figured, since you're not already calling the fire department. Emily, I'm really sorry. I'll buy you a new microwave."

"It's okay. It's not your fault this happened. Maybe it was some sort of short-circuit, and you were in the wrong place at the wrong time." *Skepticism is the greatest tool a ghost hunter has,* Emily repeated to herself.

Trevor was shaking his head, though. "No. This felt different. I've never seen a ghost. I'm not even sure I believe in them, or at least I didn't until about ten minutes ago. I've even been trying to find a rational explanation for what happened on Tuesday. Today, though, there was something, a feeling, almost like…" Trevor's voice trailed off as he brought his uninjured hand to his chest.

"The air was heavy," Emily suggested.

"Yeah. Like it was hard to breathe."

"Wait a second," Emily suddenly said. "The microwave knocked you backwards, but how did you cut your hand?"

"I put out my hands to stop my fall, and there was a nail sticking out of one of the floorboards. An indirect paranormal injury, you could say."

Emily leaned against a porch column and closed her eyes briefly. Nothing like this had ever happened before. This ghost was channeling an enormous amount of energy, and a strong entity could be a really dangerous thing, even if it wasn't intentionally hurting people. At the moment, Emily felt more fear for herself and her guests than guilt about what had happened to Trevor. Glancing at him, though, Emily saw him wince, and she felt a wave of sympathy.

"Trevor, I am just so sorry. People have never been hurt here like this. What an awful first day for you!"

Trevor gently lifted the gauze from the palm of his hand. "The bleeding has stopped," he said. "So if you've got a bandage and some anti-bacterial ointment for me, I think I'll live to work another day." He smiled at Emily, clearly trying to cheer her up.

"Okay, let's get you patched up. Then you should probably go home and change. You've smeared blood all over your shirt. I know Brianne and Nathan like spooky stuff, but I think that might be a bit over-the-top for them."

Trevor shook his head firmly. "No. No way am I

leaving you in this house by yourself. What if something happens to you, too?"

Emily tried to convince Trevor that leaving was the best option and the only possible way he could avoid getting hurt again, but he staunchly refused to go. Finally, holding up her hands in surrender, Emily agreed he could stay. "But stay out of the kitchen," she told him, "and you still have to change your shirt."

"I don't think we're the same size," Trevor said, raising an eyebrow.

Emily gave Trevor a teasing wink. "That's okay. Your prize for putting up with this ghost is your very own Eternal Rest T-shirt. In fact, I'll show you where I keep them, since I'm sure you'll wind up selling some to guests."

"You let him go home?" Sage said incredulously.

Emily had to hold the phone away from her ear. "Yes. Why not? His shift was over. I wanted him to go home right after it happened, but he insisted on staying until my guests got back so I wouldn't be alone."

"He experienced something big with the very ghost we're trying to communicate with," Sage said, her voice again at a normal volume. "Having him at the séance would have been a good idea. You invited Reed on the sole fact that some of his tools may or may not have been moved by a ghost, but you don't want the guy who had a microwave blow up on him to be a part of it?"

Emily sighed. She had known that Sage would want Trevor at the séance that night, but Emily had felt anxious to get him out of the house all day. It was bad enough that he had already been hurt one time, and she didn't want to risk anything worse happening. Asking him to attend the séance seemed like a dangerous idea to her. Maybe the ghost hadn't been trying to hurt him, and certainly there was no way to have known that Trevor would fall exactly where that popped nail was in the kitchen floor, but it still seemed risky.

Emily knew telling Sage all of that probably wouldn't do much. Instead, she simply mumbled, "Sorry. It's been a long day."

Sage's tone was sympathetic when she answered, "I know, Em. I don't like that you're having to go through this. You said Reed is coming at eight?"

"Yeah. And one of my guests, Nathan, is going to get takeout for himself and his fiancée. She'll stay here with me, so I won't be alone." Emily didn't like that idea much more than the idea of Trevor staying with her all afternoon. It seemed too much like putting innocent people in danger. Still, she had to admit to herself that she was grateful not to be alone in the house with so much unusual activity going on. Emily was even more pleased at the idea of having a full house beginning tomorrow. Maybe with more living people present, she thought, there would be less chance of paranormal activity.

Sage seemed satisfied with Emily's plan, and she promised to come over as soon as she and Jen finished dinner. She had actually offered to drop everything and come over immediately when Emily had called to fill her in, but Emily had assured her she wouldn't be alone, and it would be pointless for Sage to miss out on Jen's homemade enchiladas.

There were still a couple of hours before Reed was scheduled to arrive, so it was too early to start dinner. Emily had thrown open most of the windows on both the first and second floors to help get rid of the burning smell from the microwave. The fresh air had definitely helped with the smell, but now it was chilly inside. The heavy atmosphere that had pervaded the ground floor after

Trevor's encounter had also faded, and Emily felt reluctant to shut up the house again. Instead, she put on a heavier sweater and made herself a cup of hot tea to sip as she sat at her desk in the parlor, scrolling through some new reservation requests that had been made on the Eternal Rest website. Nathan and Brianne were upstairs in their room, but it was comforting to know they were nearby.

Reluctantly, as the last bit of daylight faded from the sky, Emily began shutting all of the windows. Again, she left a lot of lights on throughout the house to keep the shadows at bay. She was so anxious for the séance, and she was on such high alert as she listened for any odd sounds, that the minutes seemed to drag by. Ordinarily, Emily wasn't all that enthusiastic about cooking, but tonight she was grateful when it was finally time to start dinner. They would be having a chicken stir-fry: something easy that Emily was unlikely to mess up, and something that didn't require the use of a microwave. Earlier, Emily had hauled the microwave from the driveway to the brick patio behind the house, still strangely fearful of putting it on or next to anything flammable.

Emily was just adding a last dash of salt to the stir-fry when she heard a quiet knock against the kitchen doorway. "Hey," she heard Reed say. "I saw a couple of people eating in the dining room, so I just let myself in."

"Yeah, that's Nathan and Brianne, the intrepid ghost hunters staying with us through Sunday. They've already gotten more than they expected in terms of the paranormal." Emily filled two bowls and set them on the kitchen table. "Wine?"

Reed frowned. "Normally, I'd say yes, but you made it sound like we have some serious work to do tonight."

"Good point. Iced tea now, wine after the séance."

As soon as she was seated, Emily dug into her dinner. She hadn't realized how hungry she was after the stress and excitement of the day. Reed took a few slow bites, then put his fork down.

"Oh, no," Emily said around a mouthful of noodles. "Is it bad?"

"No, it's good." Reed sat back. "I promise to eat every bit of it as soon as you tell me what's going on around here. Emily, you know I believe in the supernatural. I had a great-aunt who could have given your friend Sage a run for her money. I know you believe in the supernatural, too, and you're not one to scare easily. You wouldn't call an emergency séance unless it was something pretty serious."

Emily pushed her bowl away and folded her hands on the table. "And more has happened since I spoke to you. Before today's incident, neither Sage nor I felt this ghost posed any kind of danger to us. We thought it was actually just desperate to communicate. Now, though, I'm not sure. I'm worried about what might happen tonight."

"Start from the beginning," Reed prompted.

Emily did, telling him about everything that had happened since Rhonda's dream. "I don't know if your tools moving from one spot to another even has anything to do with what's going on here in the house. I'm trying to learn to trust my instincts, like Sage says I should, and my gut was telling me to invite you here tonight."

Reed nodded his approval. "Your gut made a smart decision. You're right, what happened to me might simply be a case of one of my guys forgetting to put things away last week, or it could have been a different ghost than the one giving you problems. Regardless, having more people here tonight can only be an advantage."

Emily grimaced. "Let me guess: because there's safety in numbers?"

"In part. Also, the more observers you have, the more chances you have of detecting anything that happens during the séance. And, as I'm sure you know, ghosts need a lot of energy to do their haunting. Moving your furniture, blowing up your microwave, things like that take a lot of effort. Sometimes, ghosts will pull that energy from the living. If there are more of us at the séance, there's more energy for the ghost to tap into."

A chill ran down Emily's arms at the thought of being some sort of battery for a ghost. Still, she had to concede that Reed's points were all valid. She had known that he believed in ghosts, and now she wondered if he was a lot more knowledgeable about them than she had ever realized. She made a mental note to bring the subject up with him again sometime soon. Now, though, it was time to get the dining room ready.

As if on cue, Brianne popped her head into the kitchen. "There's a garbage can out back, right? I'm going to chuck these takeout boxes."

"To the left of the back steps," Emily answered, jerking her head in the direction of the back door. She stood and began clearing off the kitchen table, only to realize she had never finished eating. She sat back down and started to shovel the food into her mouth.

Reed just laughed. "Take your time. Let's finish eating, then I'll help you get set up for the séance. What do we need to do?"

"We just need to make sure the dining room table is clean and draw the curtains. We don't want anyone mistaking headlights from passing cars as a sign from beyond. Thanks, Reed."

Emily heard Sage arrive as she and Reed were loading their bowls into the dishwasher. Sage's voice floated down the hallway, but Emily thought she also heard a male voice that didn't sound like Nathan's. Emily was certain there was an extra voice as she got closer to the dining room, and she recognized it as Trevor's.

9

Emily stopped just inside the doorway and stood silently as fear and even a sliver of anger began to well up inside her. Sage was already laying her séance tools out on the table, including a stack of blank paper and a pencil, a purple seven-day candle, a bell, and a silver dollar. Brianne and Nathan were seated at the table, watching Sage with rapt attention. Reed moved over to the front windows, closing the curtains as he and Trevor began talking to each other quietly.

Sage didn't even look up. "I know, Em."

Emily approached the table and tried to sound nonchalant as she said, "Sage, come into the parlor with me for a minute."

Sage's face was a mixture of guilt and resolve. "This is right," she said as soon as she and Emily were in the other room.

"He could get hurt again. I didn't want him to be here tonight because I'm worried about him."

"Em, I love you, but you can be a little overprotective sometimes." Sage's voice was gentle, and she put an arm around Emily. "There are six of us here to look out for each other. Trevor might be a big help in getting this spirit to communicate tonight, and he knows better than anyone the risk he's taking by being here. He wants to help, and

I've already assured him that the second there is any sign of danger, we will shut this séance down."

There was no point in arguing about it. Emily shut her eyes and rubbed her temples. "You are so stubborn," she said. There was no anger in her voice now, just acceptance.

"I know."

"Let's get this over with."

Back in the dining room, Sage lit the candle as Emily shut the door and snapped off the lights. On the occasions she was able to participate in Sage's séances, she always took the seat closest to the light switch by the door so she only had to move a few feet in the relative darkness.

"We've all met each other already," Sage began. "Now I want you to understand how we will proceed tonight. I will attempt to call the ghost that has been causing so much activity the past few days. Our hope is to find out why it's doing this. The items on the table are tools the ghost can use to let us know they are here with us, or even to answer some questions. Ringing the bell, moving the silver dollar, or blowing out the candle are all options. Later, if I feel like we have a strong connection with the ghost, I'll try automatic writing. I'll hold the pencil over the paper, and the ghost can channel its message through my hand.

"In the meantime, I ask that you all stay as quiet as possible. However, if you sense anything, speak up—don't whisper! You don't want someone on the other side of the table to hear you whispering gossip and mistake it for a ghostly voice." Everyone laughed softly at this, and Emily knew Sage liked to use a little humor to get séance participants to relax.

"And when I say 'sense anything,' I mean every sense," Sage continued. "You can hear or see a ghost, but sometimes you can also smell them or feel them."

"And taste them?" Emily asked sardonically. Another round of laughter helped ease the mood further.

Sage's eyes were shining in the glow of the candle. "Perhaps," she said. "Tonight, though, our goal is to get answers. This is a more serious undertaking than our typical séances here. The ghosts of Eternal Rest are usually, well, restful. This unusual activity hints at a serious matter. Let's begin. Reed?"

Reed was sitting across the table from Emily, and she could hear him shift in his chair. She was still trying to figure out why Sage had unexpectedly called on him instead of diving into her normal séance routine when Reed began to speak slowly and clearly.

"Spirits of our ancestors, we call on you for your help tonight. We honor you, and we keep you in our hearts and minds, and we turn to you now for your protection and care. Please surround us with your light, love, and protection, and keep us safe from any entities that would do us harm. Please help us to assist this spirit tonight. We ask for your help, and we give you honor in return."

So many questions were running through Emily's mind. Clearly, Reed knew a lot more about the paranormal than she had realized, but how had Sage known it? She thought they had only met a few times at the house or out on the cemetery grounds. Reed had recited that prayer for protection with such assurance that Emily wondered how often he spoke it. After years of working with Reed and building a friendship with him, Emily was shocked to realize she still knew so little about him.

Before she could dwell on it any longer, Sage said, "Thank you, Reed. Now, I ask that all of you place your hands on the table, palms up."

"We're not going to hold hands?" That was Brianne's voice. She was sitting on the same side of the table as Reed, with Nathan between them.

"We are not," Sage answered. Emily could detect both amusement and impatience in Sage's voice. So many participants in Sage's séances had only seen the rituals in Victorian-era photographs, when Spiritualism was popular, or in movies. Clasping hands might have been the norm in both history and fiction, but Sage had her own preferred methods.

Sage raised her arms slightly, her hands turned up in supplication as she addressed the space above the dining room table. "My name is Sage." Her voice always changed when a séance started. It became huskier and more monotone. "I would like to communicate with the individual who is trying to convey a message to us. We have seen all of the things that you have moved. We have seen your final moments in our dreams. We are listening, and we want to help you."

Sage paused and let the silence stretch as everyone listened. Emily sat to her left, and on Sage's other side, Trevor was moving restlessly. Emily couldn't tell if he was nervous or impatient.

"Again, we are here to help you. We would like to introduce ourselves to you."

Sage's elbow bumped against Emily's, and she recognized it as her cue to speak. "My name is Emily, and this is my home," she said. "You moved everything in my bedroom, and you sent me a dream of dying while a man strangled you. I want to help you."

Reed spoke up next with, "I'm Reed, and I think you moved my tools from the barn to the cemetery. I'd like to know why."

Nathan's tone was as confident as ever. "Whatever you need to say, we are listening. My name is Nathan, and you can trust us."

After a pause, Brianne's shaking voice said, "My name is Brianne, and I had the same dream as Emily. We are so sorry for you, and we want to help you."

Trevor took a deep breath and simply said, "My name

is Trevor."

Sage paused before speaking again, clearly expecting Trevor to say something more. When it became obvious that he was finished, she said, "Now you know who we are, and we would like to know who you are. That is, of course, assuming you are truly here with us. If you are, please give us a sign. You can blow out this candle here on the table, or ring this bell. You can slide the silver dollar around. You can knock on the walls if you want. Please, if you are here, let us know."

Again a long, silent pause.

Sage repeated her invitation, but again there was no response. Emily couldn't remember ever attending a séance at Eternal Rest that didn't have some activity in the first few minutes. Usually it was something simple, like a guest feeling a cold spot or a breeze that made the candle flame flicker. For a ghost that seemed so anxious to communicate, it seemed odd that absolutely nothing was happening.

"If you're exhausted after all the things you've done in the past couple of days, you can use our energy. Draw it from us so you have the strength to communicate." Sage was trying a different tack, and Trevor drew in a sharp breath as she spoke. If he had objections, though, he didn't share them.

Again they sat in silence, and the room continued to feel absolutely normal. There were no temperature drops and the atmosphere wasn't heavy the way both Emily's bedroom and the hallway had been. A lot of times, Emily thought she could almost sense the presence of a ghost. It was like a feeling of being watched, a strange sensation that felt uncomfortable but not dangerous. Even that sensation was missing now.

Sage continued her efforts, suggesting that the ghost take the hand of anyone seated at the table. Brianne let out a startled cry at this, and the tension in the room instantly increased. Sage's tone remained level, though. "Is the ghost touching you?"

"Oh, no, sorry." Brianne sounded flustered. "I was just surprised at the suggestion, that's all."

"Mrs. Thompson?" Emily suddenly called. "Are you there? Can you hear us?"

Very quietly, as everyone strained to hear, came a faint sound, like something sliding across a surface. Emily's eyes instantly flicked to the silver dollar, but it was still in the same place on the table. As she continued listening, Emily realized the sound was coming from behind her, on the sideboard. She turned but couldn't see anything in detail so far from the reach of the candlelight.

Without stopping to consult Sage, Emily grabbed the candle from the table and held it close to the sideboard. At first, she couldn't see anything, even though the sliding noise persisted. She was about to begin looking inside the cabinets when Sage rose and pointed at a stack of china plates. The topmost plate was rotating slowly.

Silently, Sage turned and gestured at the rest of the group to get up and come look. As all six of them huddled around the sideboard, the plate gradually came to a stop, then abruptly rotated a few inches in the opposite direction.

Sage began to laugh. She reached out and lifted the top plate so everyone could clearly see the one below it. "She lined up the patterns," she said, pointing at the blue design around the rim of each plate. "Only Mrs. Thompson would be so particular. Stubborn lady."

Following Sage's cue, everyone returned to their seats around the table, and Emily replaced the candle in its rightful spot.

"Hello, Mrs. Thompson," Sage said cheerfully. "We didn't expect to see you tonight. I'm going to ask you some questions. You're good at knocking on the walls, so you can knock once if your answer is yes, and you can knock twice if your answer is no. Do you know this ghost that we are trying to contact?"

A firm knock sounded from the wall above the sideboard.

"Do you know why we haven't been able to communicate with it tonight?"

Again a single, confident knock.

Sage sighed. While yes and no questions were typically a very easy way for ghosts to communicate, they were also very limiting. It could take a long time to work out more detailed information, if it was even possible.

"Is the ghost a female?" Sage guessed.

One knock. *Yes.*

"Does she not have enough energy to communicate with us?"

Two knocks. So the ghost did have enough energy but was choosing to remain silent for some reason.

"Is she shy?"

Two knocks. It seemed like an odd question, but Emily could relate. Talking to six complete strangers could be daunting, whether or not you were dead.

"Is she angry with us?"

There was a long pause this time. Finally, there was a single soft knock on the wall. It seemed hesitant, as if Mrs. Thompson was unsure if this was the correct answer.

Sage seemed to pick up on that, and she followed up with, "Is she angry at one person here?"

But again, the affirmative knock was hesitant.

Emily thought of the hands wrapped around her neck in her dream and the darkness she had seen as she felt her life slipping away. "Scared," she said, almost more to herself than to Sage.

"I think you're on the right track, Em," Sage

murmured. "You take this one."

Emily pictured Mrs. Thompson in her mind, her white hair pulled back in a neat bun, her petite frame even smaller in her old age. She imagined Mrs. Thompson was sitting there at the table with her, and the two were enjoying a cup of coffee after the guests had all gone out for the day. "Mrs. Thompson, is this ghost scared?"

This time, the single knock was immediate and loud. A few seconds later, though, there was another knock. Emily was beginning to relax a little, assuming Mrs. Thompson had simply taken a while to get the two knocks out to indicate "no." But then there was another single knock, this time on the wall separating the dining room and the hallway.

Another knock sounded from the opposite wall.

A dull thud came from behind Nathan, as if Mrs. Thompson had slammed her fist on the window.

The knocking just kept going, one on each wall, then on the ceiling, the sounds ricocheting through the room as they began to come one right after the other. Mrs. Thompson had never behaved like this before.

Emily could see Reed across from her, his spine straight and his gazed fixed upward. Next to him, Nathan had wrapped his arms around Brianne, who had her hands clamped over her ears. Emily glanced over at Sage, who looked surprised but also excited at this outpouring of paranormal activity. Leaning forward to peer around Sage, Emily could see that Trevor appeared to be holding his breath.

Several antique paintings rattled against the walls as the knocks grew in volume. The knocks became more frequent until they were overlapping each other, and the entire room was filled with the cacophony.

Finally, there was a single loud knock right in the middle of the table. As it sounded, the candle snuffed out.

Brianne was sobbing. Everyone else was silent as they sat in the dark room, too stunned to speak. Emily roused herself enough to get up and search for the light switch on the wall. When she clicked the switch, the room looked completely normal, except for a few paintings that tilted slightly. Her shoulders relaxed as she noted that everyone seemed to be fine. Trevor was pale, and his hands were clasped tightly together. Nathan and Reed had stoic expressions, and Sage looked thoughtful. She took a few slow breaths and said, "I think that was a big 'yes' from Mrs. Thompson."

Emily snorted out a laugh. "Thank you, wise Sage. Your attitude at least lets me know that I don't need to panic about whatever just happened."

"No, I still don't think you're in danger. We're dealing with a ghost who is scared, not vengeful."

"But who is it? Is it one of our regular residents?" Emily shook her head. "I didn't think it was common for ghosts to travel from one place to another."

"They normally don't, unless they're attached to an object or a person. Have you gotten any new antique furniture lately?"

"Not for months."

"And as for your other questions, no, I don't know if it's

one of the ghosts we already know or someone new. We never actually got to communicate with her directly tonight, so we didn't get nearly as much information as I had hoped for."

Brianne had stopped crying, but she was still sniffing and wiping at her wet cheeks. "Will we be safe here tonight?" Emily felt a pang of pity for her. As much as she and Nathan said they liked visiting haunted places, experiencing something as intense as the séance had been could be jarring.

"I think so," Sage said. She spoke carefully. "I don't think you'll have any more dreams tonight. If the ghost is trying to tell us what happened to her and how we can help, it would be a waste of energy to give anyone the same dream again. We've already got that piece of the puzzle solved, so to speak. And remember, if you do have any bad dreams or if anything paranormal happens during the night, you know it's nothing meant to hurt you."

Emily glanced self-consciously down the table to Trevor, who had a big bandage across his palm. She had told her guests about the microwave incident, but she had left out Trevor's injury.

Trevor looked up at that moment and met Emily's gaze. He gave her a shaky smile. "Well, I'm not bleeding," he said.

Emily laughed again, and it felt good to have a little levity after what they had just experienced. She stood and stretched her arms over her head. Moving her body seemed like a good way to shake out the last of the fear and adrenaline. "You're all welcome to join me in the parlor for a glass of wine," she announced.

Nathan politely declined, saying a hot bath and bed would be better for Brianne. Trevor also shook his head regretfully. "I really need to get home to my dad," he said.

"Emily, are you sure you'll be okay out here by yourself tonight?"

Emily pointed to her guests, who were already heading for the staircase. "I won't be alone. Besides, I think Sage is right about this ghost not being a threat. What happened to you earlier today, I think it was just an accident. She may not have realized how much energy she was exerting."

"I hope that's the case. All right, well, I'll see you next Tuesday, then? But let me know if you need anything over the weekend." Despite his offer to help, Emily could see the relief on Trevor's face.

"I will, Trevor." Emily patted his arm. "And I'm sorry that your first day was so, um, memorable. I hope that by the time you come back, we've got this all sorted out."

As Trevor let himself out the front door, Emily retreated to the kitchen for a bottle of wine and three glasses. She was glad it was just Sage and Reed who would be joining her because she could be more frank with them.

Sage was already sprawled on the sofa when Emily came in. As she got to work with the corkscrew, she looked worriedly at her friend. She knew communicating with ghosts could sometimes be a drain on Sage's energy. Even though her eyes were closed, Sage was chatting with Reed, who had settled onto a wingback chair. His body was relaxed now, and the vigilance that Emily had sensed in him during the séance was gone. He leaned back with his legs stretched out in front of him.

Emily filled the wine glasses, and Sage didn't even open her eyes as Emily guided the stem into her fingers. Emily swatted Sage's leg. "Scoot over so I can collapse, too."

Sage leaned slightly in one direction, giving Emily space to squeeze in next to her. "You okay?" Emily asked.

"Tired, but okay. I'm really curious about what's going on here, Em. Mrs. Thompson has never acted like that!" Sage finally straightened up and opened her eyes.

"I'm worried about her. I don't like her being so agitated because of another ghost. You don't really think this is one of the Eternal Rest ghosts, do you?"

Sage shrugged noncommittally. "My best guess is that it's an outsider. I just don't know how she got here."

"Then you think Mrs. Thompson was right about it being the ghost of a woman?"

"I think it's safe to assume it's the ghost of the woman who was strangled."

"What about you, Reed?" Emily nodded in his direction. "You surprised me with that, what would you call it, a prayer?"

"That word works. I told you my great-aunt was in tune with the supernatural. She made sure she taught me how to protect myself from anything that might want to hurt me."

Emily was quiet, one hand slowly twirling her wine glass while she stared into it. Her other hand tapped against her thigh, and she chewed her lip.

Sage huffed out a breath as she leaned forward and plucked the glass out of Emily's hand. She set it down on the coffee table and took Emily's hand in hers. "It's different," Sage said firmly.

"What is? You don't even know what I'm thinking."

Sage stared at Emily, cocking her head to one side and raising an eyebrow.

Emily gave a little shrug and looked away, feeling embarrassed and a little ashamed. Of course Sage knew she had been thinking of Scott. It probably didn't even take any psychic skills to know that. Emily realized she was in a pattern of always bringing up his name after a séance, but the more paranormal activity she witnessed, the more she wanted to know if there was some way to talk to Scott. "What's so wrong with thinking of him?" she asked.

"As I'm sure Reed will confirm, our ancestors are

people from our past. We ask them to come to the present, to the moment we need their guidance or protection. You want to go the opposite way, into the past."

"I just want to talk to him," Emily said sullenly.

Sage squeezed Emily's hand, then turned her attention to Reed. She kept her fingers around Emily's, like a parent who was trying to keep a restless child still.

She doesn't understand. There are questions that no one else can answer.

Emily let the conversation between Sage and Reed fade into the background as she thought back to the days leading up to Scott's death. The crash had been completely unexpected, of course, but strangely unsurprising at the same time, almost as if she had anticipated it. Her therapist had said it was just shock, but Emily wasn't sure she agreed.

The feeling of Sage's body stiffening next to hers snapped Emily back into the present moment. Sage jerked forward in an effort to put down her wine glass, her hand shaking so badly wine sloshed over the rim. She brought the bottom of the glass down to the table, but her fingers remained tightly locked around the stem. Emily called her name as Sage's eyes, staring straight ahead, widened with panic. She made a low gurgling sound.

Emily felt her own panic rising as Sage began gasping for breath. Her mouth made little *O*s as she tried to draw in air, but it was clear she couldn't breathe.

"Stop it!" Emily screamed to the empty air around Sage. "Please, stop it!"

Reed stood and leaned over Sage, putting one hand on her back and reaching out with the other, his fingers splayed. "Stop hurting her, right now," he said in a commanding tone. "We know you were strangled. We have already received this message. We can't help you if this is all you can show us."

Suddenly, Sage coughed, and her chest heaved as air began to fill her lungs again. Her voice was raspy and so quiet Emily had to lean in to hear her. "Paper," was all she said.

"Paper?"

Sage's hand had finally released its grip on the wine glass, and she made a circular motion with her fist. "Write."

"Oh! Hang on. I'll go get it." Emily got up and ran into the dining room. Sage's pencil and sheaf of paper for automatic writing had already been packed into the bag that held her séance tools. Emily pulled them out and hurried back to the parlor, placing the loose pile of paper on the coffee table in front of Sage, not paying attention to the spilled wine that began to stain the edges of the paper red. She pushed the pencil into Sage's hand.

Sage immediately began to scrawl on the paper, forming letters with big, looping handwriting. The tip of the pencil never left the paper. As the page began to fill, Emily peered over Sage's body, bent in trance-like focus, to see the words *it's him* written over and over in one long continuous chain.

When the first page was filled, Emily hastily snatched it away so Sage could begin writing on the blank sheet underneath it, but it was still the same words.

"Is 'him' the man who murdered you?" Emily asked, her eyes darting around the room.

The words didn't change, and Sage continued writing at a feverish pace.

"Can you tell us his name?" Emily tried.

Still no change.

"Reed, you got her to stop strangling Sage, or whatever that was. Do you want to give this a shot?"

Reed repeated Emily's questions before surprising her with, "When you say 'it's him,' do you mean me?"

Emily's head snapped up to look at Reed. What kind of a question was that? It apparently didn't matter, since Sage continued scrawling the same words.

Sage was busy covering the fourth sheet of paper when her pace began to slow. Eventually, she made a final *m* and stopped, slumping forward so far her forehead touched the paper.

"Well," she said, her voice still cracking and quiet, "at least the ghost finally showed up to talk."

11

Sage had already been tired from the séance, but now she was exhausted. Emily and Reed each took an arm and helped pull her up into a sitting position. Her head lolled against the back of the sofa.

"Are you okay?" Reed put the back of one hand against Sage's forehead, like he was checking for a fever.

Sage weakly swatted at his hand. "Yup."

"This ghost needs to work on her communication skills." Emily sat back, too. "We know she was strangled, and by the way it felt in the dream, it was a man who did it. She seems to be confirming that with the automatic writing, but who is he?"

"And what does she mean by 'it's him'?" Reed asked. "Has the ghost of the man who killed her shown up? Is he going to be dangerous?"

"All good questions to ask her next time," Sage whispered.

"Oh, honey, I'm so sorry. I'll get you some water." When she went into the kitchen, Emily grabbed a handful of paper towels, too, so she could clean up the wine before it stained the wood of the table. Hopefully it hadn't already.

Emily returned and helped Sage guide the glass to her lips since her hands were trembling. Reed was walking in a slow circle around the room, deep in thought. "We know from Mrs. Thompson that this ghost is scared," he said eventually. "If the ghost of her killer has shown up here, that would be a good reason for her not just to be scared, but to be so scared that it's gotten Mrs. Thompson upset, too. They're panicking."

"But ghosts can't hurt each other, right? They're already dead." Emily looked from Reed to Sage.

"Maybe they can't hurt each other physically," Sage said, "but mentally, emotionally, sure. Imagine you're a ghost because of some horrible event—"

"Like getting strangled," Emily noted.

"Like getting strangled, and it's so bad, there's so much negative energy, that your soul is stuck here, mired in your own grief and trauma."

Emily picked up her wine glass and drained it in one gulp as Sage continued.

"Now imagine that the source of that trauma, in this case our strangler, suddenly shows up. Just his very presence must be a torment, let alone anything he might say or do."

Emily plucked the cork out of the bottle and refilled her glass. Silently, Reed held his glass out for a refill, too.

"I just hope we're able to get more information so we can properly help her," Sage continued. "I've heard of ghosts who were driven mad in the afterlife. It's not a fate anyone deserves."

"Not even a strangler?" Emily asked jokingly.

Sage rolled her head along the back of the sofa so she faced Emily. "No, not even a strangler," she said, no hint of humor in her voice.

Emily stood and started pacing behind the sofa. "But we can't help her if we don't get some better answers. We need to know *how* to help her."

"Could we banish the ghost? The strangler, I mean."

Reed glanced toward the dining room. "Is there a way to cleanse a house of just one ghost, and not all of them?"

"We could try talking to it," Sage said slowly. "It may not do much good. In fact, it might get ugly really quickly."

Emily held up a hand. "I vote that we don't make any decisions right now. We're all tired, and I'm sure we're all a little shaken up by everything that has happened tonight. Maybe after a good night's sleep we'll be able to think a little clearer. Sage, do you want to stay here tonight?"

"No, I'm feeling a bit better. I can drive home without falling asleep at the wheel."

"Okay, but text me when you get there."

"And I'll follow her as far as the square," Reed promised.

Emily extended a finger and waggled it from one friend to the other. "Someday, I want to know how you two know each other so well and how you"—her finger pointed in Reed's direction and held steady—"know so much about dealing with ghosts."

"Like I said, my great-aunt taught me well."

"Hmm." Emily narrowed her eyes, but her note of skepticism morphed into a yawn. "Okay, you two head on home. Reed, you text me, too. I want to know when you are both safe at home."

As she walked them onto the porch, Emily added, "Thank you for coming tonight. Both of you."

Sage leaned into Emily in a sort of exhausted hug. "Be careful. Wake your guests up if you need to, or call us if anything happens."

Emily gave Sage a gentle squeeze. "You two have done enough tonight. Nathan will have to be my knight in shining armor."

That finally roused a laugh from Sage.

Emily paused as soon as she shut and locked the front

door. She could hear the floorboards squeaking above her, so that meant Brianne and Nathan were still awake. She finished cleaning up the spilled wine and took everything back to the kitchen. As soon as Emily had set the glasses down on the countertop, she felt weariness wash over her. Her shoulders felt heavy, and her eyelids began to flutter. She stumbled into the bedroom and only got her jeans off before she gave up and flopped onto the bed. The lamp on the nightstand was still on, and the comforter only half covered her, but Emily was sound asleep.

Emily woke up to find sunshine streaming through her window. She rolled over so her face could soak up its warmth. It took a few minutes for her mind to reach back beyond the present bliss to the night before. Emily realized she had slept through the entire night. The last time she had slept that soundly, her room had been rearranged by the ghost. Fearing what she would find this time, Emily slowly turned her head to survey the bedroom.

Everything was exactly where it belonged. Then why did she have such a strange feeling in the pit of her stomach? It was a foreboding feeling, like something bad was about to happen. The air didn't feel heavy like it had the last time, though, and she couldn't pinpoint why the world around her felt a little out of sync. Emily listened, but she didn't hear any sounds other than the definitely human steps on the stairs.

Emily flung back the covers and made a leap for her dresser. The feeling had nothing to do with foreboding and everything to do with her subconscious brain waking up faster than the rest of her: if the sun was coming through the window at this angle, then she had overslept. Her guests were up and moving before her!

As she pulled on her usual black jeans and blue Eternal Rest shirt, Emily glanced at the alarm clock. It was a few minutes after eight. She forced herself to slow down a little. Brianne and Nathan were just now coming downstairs, and if they had to wait for the coffee to brew, then it wasn't anything to panic about. Had they been early risers like so many other guests, it would have been a different story. But with these two, Emily felt she had gotten away with her extra sleep. She had been so tired the night before that she had never even set her alarm.

Rubbing her eyes and trying to make her face look alert, Emily went into the kitchen to start the coffee and to begin piling pastries, butter, cheese, and meat on a serving tray. With only two guests, getting breakfast ready was easy. She set aside a bagel for herself.

Brianne and Nathan looked up as Emily walked into the dining room, and she found herself apologizing for the late arrival of breakfast. "We don't mind," Nathan said, leaning back in his chair. "We slept a little late, too. We were just saying how well-rested we both feel. After such a crazy séance, I expected a ghost to wake us up during the night, or that Brianne would have another dream. But I slept like the dead." Nathan snickered at his own joke. It was the same phrase printed on the Eternal Rest T-shirts that Emily sold, but she graciously chuckled as if Nathan had thought it up himself.

"What are your plans for today?" Emily asked politely.

"We're heading out to that abandoned hotel," Brianne said.

Emily was surprised to hear the excitement in her voice. After her scare during the séance, Emily had expected Brianne to want a break from the paranormal. "La-la-la-la, I didn't hear anything you just said," Emily sang teasingly, putting her hands over her ears, but then she turned serious. "I'm pretending I didn't hear you

86

because you'll be trespassing. That's private property, so enter at your own risk. You're more likely to get in trouble with the police than with any ghosts."

"We'll be careful," Nathan promised. Emily just raised an eyebrow in response. She couldn't blame them for wanting to visit the crumbling hotel. She had snuck in there plenty of times with friends during high school. They had never actually seen any evidence of ghosts, but they certainly thought they had. Every time they visited, they would run out of the place, screaming. Usually one level-headed friend would shush everyone and shout about how their noise was going to get them caught.

In fact, Emily had heard that the current owner of the property was a real estate investor in Atlanta. They wouldn't know and probably wouldn't care about anyone exploring the hotel, as long as no one got hurt. That was what worried Emily the most: that one of her guests would get hurt out there, in a place with bad cell phone reception and no one to hear a cry for help. She warned her guests about visiting the hotel more out of concern for their own safety than for any interest in the property owner or tres-passing laws.

Once Nathan and Brianne set out for their day of exploring—followed out the door by additional warnings from Emily—she quickly got their room tidied and did a quick check of the others. Check-in hours began at two o'clock, and Eternal Rest was going to be a full house until Sunday. Emily opened up the windows in all of the empty guest rooms so they would smell and feel fresh when the newcomers arrived. She enjoyed Friday mornings like this, with the promise of every room filled for the weekend giving her an extra boost of energy and optimism.

With the rooms all set, the next important thing on Emily's agenda was a shower. Once she was clean and had her still-damp hair pulled back in a low ponytail, she grabbed a feather duster and began working her way systematically through the ground-floor rooms. She always started with the parlor, feeling like the antique furnishings in there deserved a little extra time and attention.

When she reached the dining room, Emily was surprised to see a small cardboard box sitting in the middle of the table. Her first thought was that Brianne and Nathan had forgotten something of theirs, but when she got closer, she realized it was the box Reed had brought her a few days before. No, Emily corrected herself, not a few days. Sunday, nearly a week ago. She had forgotten all about it since she had been dealing with so much paranormal chaos.

Emily sat down and pulled the box toward her, her hands shaking slightly. She had left it in the kitchen. She distinctly remembered putting it on top of the microwave, back when she still had one. She had shoved the box and everything else piled on top of the microwave onto the counter following Trevor's incident in there, so how had it been moved here? The answer, of course, was a ghost, but had it been the murdered woman who moved it, or another resident?

"Only one way to find out," Emily murmured, peeling off the strip of tape Reed had put across the top.

Inside was the usual mix of things Reed found while working in the cemetery grounds. Two pennies, a quarter, a small glass bottle—at least that item looked like a cool antique that could go onto a display shelf after a thorough cleaning—and a pair of black-framed sunglasses.

As Emily lifted the sunglasses out of the box, she saw a flash of gold underneath. She gently lifted out a fine gold chain with a little heart pendant. It was a sweet necklace, and she knew someone must have been sad to lose it.

Emily peered closely at the necklace. The chain and pendant were both caked with red Georgia clay and the clasp was broken, but it was clear this was no antique. The design looked contemporary, though there was no way to tell if the necklace had been out there for a matter of weeks or years. Judging by the dirt, Emily guessed it had been waiting to be found for a long time.

Closing her hand around the necklace, Emily looked up. "Ghost?" That felt like an impolite thing to call her, but Emily wasn't sure how else to address her. "Did you put the box here so I would find this necklace?"

Emily hadn't expected any kind of an answer, not even a knock. This ghost either couldn't or wouldn't communicate so directly. She would rather blow up microwaves or send images through dreams.

Dreams. Of course. Emily gasped and sat up straight. She looked down at the necklace again. In Rhonda's dream, she said she had felt pain at her neck and someone telling her she didn't deserve fancy jewelry. Had the strangler ripped this necklace off his victim's neck before he killed her?

Reed had found it while working in the cemetery. Emily's arms broke out in goosebumps as she realized that someone had been murdered inside her own cemetery.

12

Emily was out the door and on her way to the cemetery in seconds. Luckily, Reed and his team were always at Hilltop Cemetery on Fridays to ensure the grounds looked great for weekend visitors.

Emily followed the sound of a leaf blower to the opposite side of the hill. The last leaves from the previous fall were being rounded up. Nearby, Reed was pacing back and forth along the brick path, a finger in one ear and the other pressed tightly against his cell phone.

"Yes, we can have the internment at noon on Tuesday, as long as the family is aware that we have a graveside service happening at eleven o'clock, also," he was saying. "It might be hard for everyone to find a parking space. And no, they can't have a potluck in the reception tower; it's already booked by the first family."

Reed hung up and turned to see Emily waiting for him. "Don't work in the death industry, Emily," he said gravely. "You have to deal with the living too often."

"I'll trade you. I'm dealing with the dead today, and they can be just as demanding as the living."

"Do tell."

Emily pointed to a bench one path up but nearly out of sight around the bend of the hill. "I will, but over there. It's too loud here."

Once they were settled on the bench, Emily paused for a moment to appreciate the view. The bench faced outward from the hill, and despite the magnolias and oak trees that peppered the lower part of the hillside, she could see the rolling hills on the horizon through the bare branches of the oak trees. The hills were a dark gray-blue against the crisp, pale blue of the sky.

Emily pulled the necklace out of her pocket. "What can you tell me about this?"

Reed reached out and touched the heart-shaped pendant thoughtfully. "This was over at the Clements plot. When we started removing the brick wall, we found it wedged behind a brick. I'm guessing someone lost it years ago, and over time it got covered by a layer of dirt and grass."

Emily then proceeded to tell Reed how the box appeared on the dining room table, and how the necklace seemed to be the most likely connection to the ghost's story. She ended with, "I think it's very possible that a woman was murdered here in the cemetery."

Reed nodded slowly. "It is possible," he conceded. "The only thing within shouting distance of the cemetery is your house. And if you had a houseful of guests, you wouldn't necessarily notice any commotion out here."

Emily shuddered and instinctively wrapped her arms around herself. "Do you think I was home when it happened? I could have been a hundred yards away from a murder."

"We have no way of knowing that, so there's no point worrying about it. What we need to be thinking about is how we can use this knowledge to help your ghost. Let's say your instinct is right, and this necklace was ripped off her neck right before she was strangled. While it seems likely it happened here in the cemetery, where the necklace was found, it might have happened elsewhere, and the necklace was buried out here on purpose."

"It seems like a strange place to get rid of evidence." Emily suspected Reed was only suggesting this to make her feel better.

"Agreed. I'm just trying to look at other possibilities. If you jump right to the conclusion that someone was murdered here at Hilltop, then you might be so focused on that theory that you miss other important signs from the ghost."

Emily had to agree. "I should keep my mind open to other possibilities. You're right, but I do think we should ask the ghost if she was killed here. Maybe she'll actually give us a firm answer this time around."

"Maybe, but the way she's been so far, I doubt it." Reed watched as two women in exercise clothes jogged past. Locals liked going there for the pretty scenery, and they didn't seem to mind getting fit at a cemetery. Reed and Emily both nodded and smiled politely. "That reminds me," he said, "I saw a man in here this morning."

"That's not unusual. Lots of people come here."

"I know, Emily, but there was something about him that made me uncomfortable. I didn't get a good look at him because he had on a hat and sunglasses, and his scarf nearly came up to his nose. He was coming down the hill as I was unlocking the gate. That in itself isn't a big deal. Lots of early-morning walkers and joggers will just hop the wall if the gate is closed, but this didn't seem like someone out for their health. When he saw me, he actually turned down one of the ring paths, and I never saw him again. I think he wanted to avoid being seen."

Emily glanced nervously over her shoulder, as if she expected to see the stranger looming behind the bench. *Calm down*, she told herself. *Don't jump to conclusions.*

Instead of taking her own advice about that, she said,

"We've been assuming that 'it's him' meant that the ghost's killer was now haunting Eternal Rest, too, but what if he's still alive?"

"I thought of that, too, but honestly, I think it's just a coincidence. I do think, however, you should keep a close eye on this place. Whatever his reason for being here was, no one lurks around an old cemetery just for fun. It could have been a hitchhiker who slept here last night, or maybe he was out here for some kind of illicit business."

Emily actually laughed at that suggestion. "What, like he's part of the Oak Hill mafia or something?"

"I was thinking more along the lines of selling drugs, but I like your flair for the dramatic." Reed was laughing, too. He stood and straightened his City of Oak Hill sweatshirt. "Just keep an eye out, okay?"

"I will. And you, too! When you get to work again on the Clements plot, please let me know if you find anything else."

"You'll be the first to know. We're going to do some more leveling beginning Monday. I hope we can have the foundation in place by the end of next week."

Emily wished Reed a good weekend before adding with a grin, "And if you come visit your family plot on Sunday, you know I'll have a croissant for you!"

The first weekend guests arrived promptly at two. The party of four women said they were in town for the antiquing. They loved historic homes, and they were more interested in the architectural details of Eternal Rest than its ghosts. They had just settled into the parlor with iced teas when the next guests arrived. This was a couple from Florida who had family in Oak Hill but, as they explained, it was a lot easier to love your family when you weren't staying under the same roof with them.

After the flurry of arrivals, the house suddenly felt very empty as the two parties headed into town for the afternoon. The women planned to visit a few antique stores on the edge of town, and the couple left to visit relatives.

Emily mulled over Reed's warning about the stranger in the cemetery as she sat at her desk. Reed had probably been right that there was no connection between that man and this new ghost, but Emily made a mental note to ask the ghost about it at the next séance. The next Spirited Saturday Night weekend was still another three weeks away, but Emily knew Sage would want to come out a lot sooner than that. Hopefully on Sunday night, once the house was empty again.

Brianne and Nathan came back from the abandoned hotel around four, and they gleefully regaled Emily with their adventure there, which included a video with what Nathan insisted was a ghost in it. "You can see this orb that moves across the room, like it's a person walking from one doorway to the other," he enthused.

"Wow," Emily said, trying to sound supportive. She was skeptical of orbs, the bright balls of light that sometimes showed up in photos and video. Often, they were nothing more than bugs or dust motes that were caught at just the right angle in the flash of the camera or the beam of a flashlight. She was the last person who would try to dampen the spirits of her own guests, though.

"How was your day?" Nathan asked, his tone switching to one of concern.

Emily considered telling him and Brianne about the box and the necklace, but for some reason she just didn't feel willing to disclose that information. She hadn't even told Sage yet. Emily wasn't sure why she felt that way, though she suspected having to admit someone was possibly murdered in her own cemetery had something to do with it.

"I spent a nice morning out in the cemetery," Emily finally said. It wasn't a lie.

Nathan nodded. "We're planning to explore every inch of it tomorrow morning. We'll stick close to home for the day."

As Nathan and Brianne headed upstairs to their room, Emily returned to her desk, but the doorbell rang just as she sat. It was Trish from Grainy Day Bakery, balancing a big box of baked goods with one arm while she spoke incredulously into a cell phone. "I'm all for making a fun cake for a bachelorette party, but that's taking it a bit far, don't you think? We have some fun phrases we can write on the cake and even some bachelorette cake toppers, but do you really want the cake to be in the shape of—oh, Em, one sec—anyway, think about some alternative cake styles you'd like and get back to me, okay? Bye!"

Trish rolled her eyes. "My soon-to-be sister-in-law," she explained in a thick Southern accent as she pushed the box into Emily's hands. Trish was petite, with bright blue eyes and blonde hair that was always pulled back in a French braid. She was a year older than Emily, but she looked much younger.

"I'm surprised to see you so early today!" Emily said. Trish usually stopped by Eternal Rest with the next morning's order after she closed up her bakery, since she had to pass the house on her way home. It was a convenient arrangement for Emily, and it wasn't out of the way for Trish.

Trish waved an arm. "Clint is finally old enough to keep an eye on the place once he gets out of school. I'm just running home to change my shirt. I've been wearing my jacket and sweating my butt off for hours because I didn't want customers to see this." Trish dramatically unzipped her jacket and held it open. The white T-shirt underneath had a deep red stain right over her heart.

"Trish! You should be at the hospital!" Emily nearly dropped the box as she stepped back and turned her eyes away.

"Exactly! You can see why I had to hide this. But don't worry, it's not blood. There was a little food-coloring accident."

Emily let out a breath. "You scared me. At least you don't need to worry about finding a costume when Halloween comes around."

"Oh, no, this is going right in the trash. I don't want to run around looking like a murder victim."

Emily grimaced at that last part. She had been thinking enough about murder today.

Trish turned to go and was already starting to wave goodbye when she paused, turned back to Emily, and leaned in conspiratorially. "Hey, what do you know about Trevor Williams? Remember him? He's back in town, and he looks *good*!"

"He was just here yesterday," Emily said, wiggling her eyebrows suggestively. Her laugh ruined the joke. "He works here, actually. He was looking to pick up some extra cash, and I've needed help since Mrs. Thompson died. You know Trevor moved back here to take care of his dad, right?"

"That old beast." Trish groaned. "Yes, I know, he's sick. But old habits die hard."

"I know. I used to feel the same way about him. I saw him this week, though, and he seems like a nice man. Dillan and Trevor might have exaggerated a little bit about how mean their dad was."

"Probably. Clint exaggerates about me, I'm sure. His whole class probably thinks I'm a monster, too." Trish opened her jacket again. "See? I'm so awful that somebody shot me right through the heart!" She laughed and waved again. "See you tomorrow!"

Emily waved back. Trish had always been a little overly dramatic, and getting her daily delivery of baked goods was never a dull experience. Just as she was turning to go inside, Emily heard Trish shout, "It's going to rain tonight! Bring those clothes in!"

Emily had already shouted back her thanks before she realized she had no idea what Trish was talking about. There was an old clothesline in the backyard, but Emily only ever used it for the bed sheets. And even if she did have her clothes hanging on it, it wasn't visible from the driveway. Curious, Emily dropped the box of baked goods inside the front door and walked around to the side of the house. There, on the grassy stretch between the house and the cemetery wall, items of clothing were scattered as if someone had been throwing them out of the upstairs windows. They formed a loose line that snaked in the direction of the cemetery.

As Emily walked closer, she quickly realized that none of the clothes belonged to her. They were all women's clothing, but the assortment of blouses, skirts, and dresses must belong to one of the women staying at Eternal Rest that weekend.

Emily had closed the upstairs windows after airing the rooms, but as she looked up now, she could see that the window of the rearmost room on this side of the house was wide open. The screen was lying on the junipers directly below the window.

"Not cool!" Emily shouted. Maybe the ghost was trying to send another message, but all she felt in that moment was anger. These belonged to one of her guests, and now Emily would have to apologize and explain that an impetuous ghost had thrown them all out the window. Besides, she already knew the cemetery played some role in the ghost's murder, so why point her in the direction of the cemetery again? Or, Emily speculated, maybe that wasn't what the ghost was trying to communicate at all.

Emily got to work gathering up each item of clothing, pausing every now and then to huff out a breath angrily or to mumble, "This is ridiculous!" Thankfully, everything seemed to be clean and undamaged. Since the grass was still the brown, dead blades of winter, there were no grass stains on the white blouse. On a hunch, Emily also carefully searched the ground for jewelry. She wasn't surprised to find a string of pearls and a few bracelets. Hopefully she wasn't overlooking anything smaller.

Once the clothes were all neatly folded and stacked on the dining room table, Emily stomped into the hallway and shouted, "Do *not* interfere with my guests! You can talk to me, but not to them. They are *off limits*! But if you're going to talk to me, you have to be more clear, because I don't even know what you're trying to tell me!"

Emily started at the sound of footsteps above her. Was the ghost actually going to respond? Then a man's voice hesitatingly called, "Emily? Everything okay?"

Emily put her head in her hands and groaned as she felt the heat rising in her cheeks. She had completely forgotten that Nathan and Brianne were upstairs.

"Yes," she called up. "Just laying some ground rules."

Nathan came downstairs looking concerned. "You sounded really upset."

Emily shrugged and gestured toward the dining room. "Go see what I just collected from the side yard."

Nathan let out a whistle as he surveyed the clothes. "Somebody dumped clothes in your yard?"

"Somebody"—Emily emphasized the word—"threw them all out of a guest room window."

"Why?"

"Your guess is as good as mine. They were sort of in a line leading toward the cemetery, but that could just be a coincidence."

"We'd be happy to do a little investigating out there tomorrow. I can take my tape recorder. In fact, if you'll let us in there tonight, we can try to get some photos or even video of the ghost."

Emily thought for a while. It wasn't a bad idea. Brianne and Nathan were certainly enthusiastic about helping her with this haunting, and she hated to turn down the offer of assistance. Reed's warning was still fresh in her mind, though. Emily didn't want them to meet anyone suspicious out there, especially not at night.

"I'll go with you," she said, her mind made up. "We'll go late, when the other guests aren't likely to need anything from me. We'll set up by the Clements plot."

"Okay," Nathan said doubtfully. "Why there?"

Emily still didn't want to tell Nathan about the necklace. Instead, she said, "The wall around that plot is being rebuilt. Maybe the work is stirring up some of this paranormal activity."

By the time Emily was alone again, she had made up her mind that even if she was reluctant to tell Nathan the full story, Sage at least needed to hear it. Emily went into her bedroom and shut the door to get as much privacy as possible before pulling out her cell phone.

Sage was less concerned about a possible murder in the cemetery and more excited about the necklace. "The ghost must have been tied to the necklace, and finding it woke her up, spiritually speaking. This helps us," she enthused. "We're doing a séance out there by the Clements plot."

"Nathan and Brianne want to do some ghost hunting in the cemetery tonight. Want to come over so we can do a séance, too?"

"No, it's going to storm tonight. Let's plan for tomorrow."

Emily agreed, and she spent the rest of the evening alternating between nervousness and relief. She was nervous about what might happen in the cemetery during the impromptu ghost hunt with Nathan and Brianne, but she was also relieved to have relayed everything to Sage. Laying out all the details put it into better perspective. Yes, it was sad that someone might have been murdered in the cemetery, but since there were already so many dead bodies there, maybe she had been overreacting to the idea. Emily didn't know if her ghost hunters would learn anything useful, but she absolutely expected Sage to get some results during the séance. Emily felt reassured that she was going to get some answers, one way or another.

Emily made sure that everything was as prepped as possible for breakfast the next morning before she started getting ready for the cemetery. She knew she was going to be up way past her bedtime, and she didn't want to roll out of bed the next morning a minute earlier than she had to. She also peeked into room number three, the one that had been raided by the ghost, to ensure that everything else was in place.

The couple who was visiting family came back shortly after dinnertime, but the four women who had gone out in search of antiques didn't get back to the house until nearly eleven o'clock. They admitted that after shopping at a few antiques stores and having dinner, they decided to visit Oak Hill's sole bar. Emily had guessed that already from all of the giggling and flushed cheeks.

She hated to bring down the mood of the friends with her news about the clothes, but she waved them into the dining room anyway. "Whose clothes are these?"

"Mine," chorused two women.

"You're both in room number three? The one at the back?" Emily pointed upstairs.

They nodded.

"I'm so sorry, but it seems that one of the ghosts here, um, well, she took an interest in your clothes. I found them on the lawn outside your window."

All four women stared at Emily with wide eyes and open mouths. They were shocked into silence for a heartbeat, and then they all began talking at once. Emily had a hard time keeping up, but mostly they seemed excited. She let out a breath she didn't realize she'd been holding.

Emily emphasized that the clothes weren't damaged at all, and she showed them the jewelry, asking if any other pieces were missing. The women staying in room three shook their heads. "The rest of it is on me," one of them said, waggling her ring-bedecked fingers.

"Good. But please take a close look when you get upstairs, and let me know if anything is missing or damaged. I promise I'll pay to replace anything, if necessary." Emily mentally crossed her fingers that everything would be accounted for: judging by the one woman's rings, she couldn't afford such a bold promise.

Emily's guests were unconcerned about her upcoming trip to the cemetery, and they all assured her they wouldn't need anything from her in the middle of the night, anyway. Now, if they would all just go to bed, Emily could actually finish getting ready to go.

One of the women laid a hand on Emily's shoulder while the rest trooped upstairs, already back to giggling. "I grew up in a haunted house," the woman said reassuringly. "Don't you worry about a couple of clothes getting tossed out the window. You have nothing to be afraid of."

Emily thought about telling her that paranormal activity was nothing new at Eternal Rest and she wasn't scared but angry. But when the woman let out a loud belch and giggled, Emily figured it wasn't worth the effort.

Finally, the house began to quiet down. Emily still heard heavy footsteps and muffled laughter from upstairs as she pulled on a sweatshirt and fished her old hiking boots out of the wardrobe. She hadn't gone hiking since she and Scott had taken a vacation in the mountains the year before he died, and now they only came out when Emily was accompanying ghost hunters in the cemetery.

On a hunch, Emily also retrieved the gold necklace and tucked it into her jeans pocket. If the ghost was tied to the necklace itself, it might help them communicate tonight.

As planned, Brianne and Nathan met Emily at the bottom of the stairs promptly at midnight. Emily had put on a jacket and a scarf, and she had grabbed a flashlight. Nathan, she noticed, had an entire backpack of equipment, and he carried a tripod in one hand.

"Ready to look for ghosts?" she asked. Nathan emphatically nodded, but Brianne just gave a slight shrug. Emily couldn't blame her for being a little uneasy after what had happened at the séance. Turning toward the hall, Emily announced, "We're going to the cemetery. If you want to communicate, come with us. We'll even have a tape recorder for you to talk into."

Outside, the wind was rattling the branches of the oak tree in the front yard, and it made a faint moaning sound as it sped past the parlor chimney. Trish and Sage had been right: it was going to storm. Emily zipped up her jacket and hoped they could get some investigating done before it started raining, though it would be a wonder if they could hear any ghostly voices over the sound of the wind.

Clicking on her flashlight, Emily carefully led the way to the front gate. The hinges creaked as she swung it open, sounding extra spooky at this time of night and in this weather. From there, the three walked up the hill to the Clements plot.

"What now?" Emily asked.

"I'm going to set up the tripod so my video camera points right at that area they're working on," Nathan explained. "Then we can sit and do an EVP session."

EVP sessions were, to Emily, incredibly boring. The idea of sitting in the dark with a tape recorder, asking questions of a ghost but not ever expecting to hear an answer, just seemed silly. Of course, Emily knew the ghost hunters hoped they would hear a ghost's answers on the recordings when they played them back later, since electronic devices seemed to be able to pick up things that human ears couldn't. Even when an EVP session yielded crisp words from an unseen entity, that didn't change the fact that the work that went into getting it was less interesting than washing dishes, as far as Emily was concerned.

Brianne was the one handling photography, and she was already snapping away with her camera. Nathan was struggling to secure the tripod, which would shake every time a gust of wind blew down the path. He eventually resorted to sitting right next to it with his left arm wrapped around one of the legs to hold it steady. Brianne and Emily sat down on the path next to him so they were all facing the Clements plot.

With his right hand, Nathan hit the "record" button on his tape recorder and placed it on the ground in front of them. "We are beginning an EVP session at Hilltop Cemetery. Please, no whispering. If you want to say something, say it clearly. And to you"—now Nathan's voice grew louder as his gaze turned toward the plot—"we invite you to come say anything you like into my tape recorder here. What is your name?"

Nathan went through the standard list of questions, asking the ghost how old she was, when she had died, who had killed her, and even if she would be so kind as to pose for Brianne and her camera.

The entire time, the wind continued to pick up. Brown leaves were skittering down the path, and small branches were beginning to fall from the trees above them. "We won't have much longer," Emily announced after half an hour of Nathan's questions.

"Do you want to ask anything?" Nathan gestured to give Emily the go-ahead.

"Is this where you were killed?" she asked. She saw the surprised glances from her companions out of the corner of her eye, but she continued staring at the spot where the brick wall used to be, where the necklace had been found. After a pause, Emily added, "Is your killer here with us, too?"

Just then, there was a bright flash of lightning. The thunder followed immediately, making the ground tremble slightly. In the brief moment that the cemetery was lit up, Emily saw the form of a man walking up one of the narrow paths between monuments. As the darkness closed around them again, she stood abruptly. "We're going. Now."

Without waiting for a response, Emily snatched the video camera and tripod and began walking. Nathan shouted as he quickly unwound his arm from the tripod leg so he wouldn't get pulled along, too. Hastily, he and Brianne followed Emily.

Emily swept her flashlight from left to right constantly as they hurried back to the house. There were more flashes of lightning, but Emily didn't see the man again. Reed's strange encounter and his warning heightened her urgency to put distance between herself and the dark figure.

The first fat drops of rain were beginning to fall as they reached the porch. Emily hurried Brianne and Nathan inside, locked the door, and ushered them into the dining room. She shut the door behind them so they wouldn't bother the guests upstairs.

"You really don't like lightning," Brianne said, slightly out of breath.

"It wasn't the lightning that made you want to leave," Nathan said slowly, his eyes narrowed at Emily, "was it?"

"Did you see him, too?" Emily realized her voice was shaking.

Nathan rubbed his chin absently. "I thought I saw

something. I couldn't tell what it was, but it was like a dark shadow to the left of the Clements plot. I wasn't looking directly at it when the lightning flashed, so I only saw it out of the corner of my eye."

Emily flopped down into a chair. "I was looking right at it. It looked like a man walking up the path."

"Why did you leave so quickly?" Brianne sounded a little scared now. "If it was a ghost, wouldn't you want to speak with it?"

Emily leaned back and gazed up at the ceiling thoughtfully. Why had she been so overwhelmed by the need to get out of there? If she had been alone, she probably would have run all the way back to the house. Had she simply been startled? Did she feel threatened by the mysterious visitor?

"I don't know," Emily finally conceded. "I didn't really think; I just acted." Sage would have been proud of her for following her instincts.

"Do you think it was a ghost?" Brianne asked.

Did she? "No," Emily said thoughtfully. "Reed saw a suspicious man leaving the cemetery early this morning. I think it's more likely that someone is currently making Hilltop their home, or they're using it as a place to do things they want to keep secret."

Nathan had been staring at the tiny screen on his video camera, and he made a frustrated noise. "No luck getting video evidence. I had the camera zoomed so tightly on the Clements plot that the walkway to the left of it isn't in the shot at all. That's disappointing."

There was another flash from outside, and a loud clap of thunder sent a shudder through the house.

"At least you have the tape to review, not to mention the rest of the video," Emily said, trying to sound optimistic.

"We'll start reviewing them as soon as we're up tomorrow," Nathan promised.

Emily wished them a good night, staying in her chair as she listened to them quietly ascending the stairs. Any tiredness she had felt earlier had disappeared. Her heart seemed to be returning to a normal speed, and she could tell her brain was retreating from panic, but she still felt uneasy. The idea that a ghost had come to visit them at the cemetery really didn't scare her.

The idea that a living person had been stalking toward them in the middle of the night, in the dark, terrified her.

14

Emily put the tray of baked goods down on the sideboard and stared at it for a moment. It felt like something was missing, but her foggy brain couldn't figure out what it was. She blinked a few times, tried to concentrate on the tray again, and finally gave up, heading back to the kitchen for more coffee. None of her guests were downstairs yet, and judging by the silent floorboards above her head, none of them had even made it out of bed. Emily made a mental note to adjust the breakfast hours for Sunday morning, when she might be able to sleep in a bit, too.

The storm had raged for hours. The rain had stopped by five in the morning, something Emily only knew because she had been awake yet again at that hour. All night long she had alternated between a troubled sleep, in which a dark form that resembled a man was walking toward her in the dark, and waking up to worry that someone was standing outside her window.

Emily wondered how many cups of coffee it would take before she had enough energy to go outside and look for any damage from the storm.

A buzz emanated from Emily's phone. It was a text from Sage that read, *Come let me in.*

Frowning, Emily walked skeptically to her front door. Sage was never out and about this early. But when she opened the door, Sage stood there with an insulated coffee cup in one hand and her bag of séance instruments in the other.

"Isn't it too early for a séance?" Emily mumbled.

"I'm staying here with you all day," Sage answered firmly.

The note of concern in Sage's voice woke Emily up a bit more. "But Saturdays are your busiest days at your shop."

"People can wait to communicate with their dead loved ones. Today we're going to work on communicating with your ghost." Without waiting for a response, Sage pushed her way past Emily and headed toward the kitchen. "But I need more coffee first."

Sage was already refilling her mug when Emily shuffled in behind her. As they sat down at the kitchen table, Sage remarked on the quietness of the house. "I didn't ring the bell because I didn't want to wake anyone, but I didn't expect everyone to sleep in."

"I've got four ladies who wound up at Sutter's last night, a couple trying to avoid too much time with relatives, and Nathan and Brianne, who I went to the cemetery with."

"Yeah, about that," Sage said, putting her mug down with a *thunk*. "I think you stirred something up last night. I'm part of the dream club now. Instead of being strangled, though, I heard an odd repetitive noise that made me think of a scratched record. I couldn't see anything, so I have no idea where I was. When I woke up, I had the distinct feeling that I should be out here with you."

"I appreciate the company. I might let you watch the house while I take a nap later."

"Put some cucumber slices on your eyes when you do. You look rough."

"Wow, thanks for the support."

"Now tell me why you look like you got about five minutes of sleep the entire night."

Emily launched into her experience at the cemetery the night before, and Sage looked concerned as Emily described seeing the form that could have been either a real man or simply the ghost of one.

"This could support the theory that her killer is here." Sage began to tick off points on her fingers. "We know she's scared, she wrote 'it's him' during our automatic writing session, the clothes in the side yard seemed to point to the cemetery, and then this guy shows up last night."

Emily raised a hand. "Agreed, except we don't know if this killer is alive or dead. We also don't know if what I saw last night was just a normal person who has nothing to do with any of this. I guess I need to look into video cameras for the cemetery, too. I thought having them on the house was enough."

"Talk to Reed. I bet you can get the city to pay for it."

As Emily and Sage continued to talk, the guests slowly began to stir above them. The ladies from room three were the first to come downstairs. They thanked Emily multiple times when she brought the coffee to them in the dining room.

"We double-checked, and everything is still in its place," said one. "We're going to be gone all day, so we wanted to ask if you have a safe where we can put our jewelry."

"Of course." Emily was relieved that even with clear heads, the women weren't upset about the paranormal activity. "Butter!" she suddenly shouted.

The women looked like they weren't sure whether they should laugh or be concerned by Emily's outburst. Emily sheepishly pointed at the tray of baked goods. "I knew something was missing earlier, and I just realized it's the butter. I'll go get it for you."

The other two ladies trailed into the room soon after, and by ten they were all heading out the door to go antiquing. The couple visiting family left right on their heels. Once they were gone, Emily and Sage made a circuit of the exterior of the house, but nothing more than some branches had fallen victim to the storm. The ground was soggy, and there were big puddles in the lower areas of the yard, which meant the cemetery would also be a swampy mess.

Emily was sipping yet another cup of coffee when she heard rapid footsteps coming down the stairs. Her first thought was that something was wrong, and she dashed into the hallway. But Nathan's face was the opposite of panicked: he was grinning. "You're going to love this!" he shouted, waving his tape recorder. Brianne followed at a slower pace, but she was also smiling broadly.

Everyone gathered around the tape recorder, which Nathan set on the coffee table in the parlor. "I got nothing," he said, looking at Emily excitedly. "There were no answers to my questions, and the wind was so bad that I was starting to think the whole EVP session would be a bust. Then you started talking."

Nathan started the already-cued tape, and Emily heard her own voice say, "We won't have much longer." A quiet, feminine voice responded.

Emily leaned forward, her eyes wide. "Who was that? What did she say?"

Nathan pulled a pair of earbuds from his pocket. "Listen to it with these."

Emily put the earbuds in and closed her eyes in concentration while Nathan rewound the tape. This time, "We won't have much longer" boomed into her ears, followed by a distinct answer of "not long now."

"Whoa." Emily knew her face must look like her guests' shocked faces the night before when she had told them about the thrown-out clothing. "That voice is clear as day."

Sage took a listen next, and she nodded her head in approval. "Well done, you three. See, Emily, I told you I woke up feeling like I needed to be here with you. Something is going to happen, and it's going to happen soon."

"But I was referring to the storm in that recording, saying we wouldn't have much time to investigate. Don't you think this voice is just agreeing with me?"

"No. I think everything we've experienced so far this week was just a warm-up for something bigger."

Emily turned to her guests as she tried to suppress a shudder. "Are you still planning to explore the cemetery after all that rain?"

Nathan and Brianne both nodded eagerly. Emily was glad to see that Brianne's enthusiasm for the paranormal had returned to its previous level, before she had been so upset at the séance. "We're going to try another EVP session," Nathan said. "Do you want to come with us? You were the only one the ghost responded to last night."

"Actually, I am going with you, but not for a ghost. I need to take a quick look to see if the storm did any damage. Reed and his team won't be out again until after the weekend, and I want to make sure the paths are clear and that none of the monuments have damage." Emily stood as she stifled a yawn. "Sage, you should come, too. I suppose Mrs. Thompson can watch the house for a bit."

Emily put on a pair of rain boots and grabbed her gardening gloves before they all walked over together. She expected more than a few downed branches that would have to be moved.

It took more than twenty minutes to walk from the cemetery gate to the top of the hill because they kept stopping to move branches. A few were so large it took two people to drag them to the side of the path. Nathan and

Brianne were clearly anxious to get started on their EVP session at the Clements plot, but even they stayed to help with the clearing up. There were a few large puddles on the brick paths, but no signs of damage to the grave markers or mausoleums.

When they reached the top of the hill, Emily and Sage began working their way down the far side of it, though there seemed to be fewer branches crisscrossing the ground there. Nathan and Brianne went back down the path to start their work at the Clements plot.

It didn't take long for Emily to declare the entire cemetery safe for visitors, so she and Sage made the walk to the other side of the hill once again to see how the EVP session was going. *For someone who slept so little,* Emily thought wryly, *I sure am getting a lot of exercise this morning.*

As they neared the Clements plot, Emily could see that Nathan and Brianne were both crouched on the ground, peering closely at the strip of dirt between the edge of the path and the spot where the brick wall was being rebuilt.

Neither one of them looked up as Emily and Sage approached. The first thing that popped into Emily's mind was that more jewelry had been discovered. She leaned over their kneeling forms and tried to figure out what had caught their attention. "What are we looking at?"

Nathan pointed to something lumpy that was protruding about half an inch out of the ground. It was about six inches long, and even though it was stained the rusty orange of the clay in which it sat, it clearly had a slight texture to it. "It looks like an animal's hide," Nathan said. "We think maybe an animal was buried here a long time ago. The rain washed away so much dirt that it's on the surface now."

Emily squatted down, her eye catching something dark blue on one end of the strange object. She slid on her gardening gloves, not willing to touch a dead animal with her bare hands, and carefully scratched away some of the dirt and clay. Whatever the blue spot might be, it was thin, and Emily hooked one finger under it and tugged. The object was soft, but it wouldn't move, so she began to wiggle it until it slowly began to rise out of the ground. The part that looked like animal hide came with it, clearly attached.

With a nervous laugh, Emily said, "It's just a jacket sleeve. Someone probably left it out here ages ago, and it got buried over the years. See, the part that you said looked like animal hide is exactly that, Nathan. It's leather."

"A leather sleeve with a blue cuff," Sage said flatly. "An Oak Hill High School letterman jacket."

"Some drunk high schooler probably left it out here during a party." Emily shook her head in distaste. She grasped the sleeve and gave it a hard yank in an effort to free the jacket from the muddy ground. Nathan leaned in and grabbed the shoulder as it emerged, adding to the effort.

"I don't think we should be doing this," Sage said, her voice suddenly higher than usual. "Em, this isn't a good idea."

"Why not?" Emily stopped pulling and looked at Sage with concern. When Sage had a hunch, it was usually best to go with it. Emily had learned that over their many years as friends.

Nathan was now leaning backward, using his body weight in a strange tug-of-war with the ground. Just as Sage opened her mouth to answer Emily, the mud finally yielded its prize, the suddenness of it sending Nathan tumbling backward with the jacket on top of him.

Brianne screamed, but she wasn't looking at Nathan. Her eyes were fixed on the bones that were now scattering across the path.

15

The brittle little bones had flown out of the jacket when it popped out of the ground. They tumbled across the brick path, tapping out a horrifying tune.

Nathan threw the jacket away from him and heaved himself up from the ground. Emily had dropped down onto her knees, her hands pressed against her face as the gardening gloves left red streaks of clay down her cheeks. Brianne was sobbing hysterically. Only Sage was silent, her face pale and her eyes shut tight.

Emily fought to have some kind of coherent thought. She looked down at the bones that had landed near her. *Maybe*, she tried to tell herself, *it's just an animal. Maybe some high schooler's dog died, and they buried it out here, wrapped in the jacket.* But those ribs were too big to be a dog's. And that long, thin bone that was half-in, half-out of the jacket sleeve hadn't come from anyone's pet.

"Okay," Emily said, spreading her hands wide. "We all just need to stay calm. We need to call the police."

No one moved.

"Okay," she tried again, "I'm calling the police. Nathan, take Brianne away from this, but don't go far."

As Nathan guided his fiancée away from the body and somewhat out of earshot, Emily stripped off her gloves and pulled out her phone. Her hands shaking, she dialed nine-one-one and waited while her brain ran through a hundred possible scenarios. Every plausible explanation came back to one single fact: there was a dead body in her cemetery that wasn't supposed to be there.

Later, Emily wouldn't even be able to recall her conversation with the dispatcher. She only knew that she still had the phone pressed against her ear when she began to hear the sirens. As two police cars and an ambulance pulled up, Emily wondered why they would bother bringing an ambulance for someone who was so obviously already dead. A giggle erupted from her lips, and she slapped her hand over her mouth to stop it. She turned to Sage, who was still standing there with her eyes closed. Without opening them, Sage reached out and clasped Emily's hand.

Emily walked toward the cemetery entrance in a daze to lead the police to the Clements plot. At some point, as she was relaying what had happened, she felt Sage gently pry her cell phone out of her hand. After a flurry of questions, the police turned their attention to the bones and the spot in the ground that Emily now knew had been a shallow grave. Gradually, her shock began to wear off and she started to recognize the gravity of the situation.

Emily's stomach lurched. She turned away and bent double as she felt bile rising in her throat. She tried to breathe deeply, her hands braced against her thighs, praying she wouldn't throw up in front of all these people. She felt a firm, comforting hand on her back, but the voice attached to it was shaking. "Emily, what's going on? Did someone sneak in here and dig up a grave?"

It was Reed. Emily forced herself to stand up and face him. She tried to speak but couldn't. Instead, she shook her head.

"But those are human bones," Reed countered.

Emily nodded. She took another deep breath, and this time she was able to force the words out of her mouth.

"The body was just under the surface. If your team had dug just a little wider for the wall, you probably would have found it. I think the storm last night washed away the last of the dirt that was covering it."

Emily shook her head before continuing. "I don't understand. That woman's ghost led us here. It was her necklace that was found here. But in my dreams, she wasn't wearing a jacket. Her arms were bare. So if the body isn't hers, then whose is it? And was their death somehow related to hers?"

Reed turned and looked at the spot grimly. The Clements plot was now a crime scene, and already the police were cordoning off the area. Sage, who had been hunched over the letterman jacket, stood up and said something quietly to one of the officers. They spoke for a few moments as he furiously wrote in a small notebook, then Sage walked toward Emily and Reed. Emily had never seen her friend looking so pale and weak. So vulnerable. That was almost more frightening than the body. Sage was always the tough one, never fazed by anything that got thrown at her by the living or the dead. Now, she looked defeated.

Sage took Emily's hand again. "There's a name embroidered on the jacket," she said, her voice husky as if she had been crying. "Dillan."

Emily rocked back on her feet, stunned. "Oh, no," she said, her eyes darting to the jacket. "Oh, no, no, no, no, no."

"That means something to you?" Reed asked. He put a steadying hand on Emily's back again.

"Dillan Williams. He went missing when we were in high school. Everyone thought he'd just skipped town."

"Oh." Reed swallowed hard. "I remember hearing about that."

Sage began to cry. The crumpled expression looked so

out of place on her face, and it just made Emily feel worse. She pulled Sage into a tight hug and rocked her back and forth slowly. "It will be okay," she soothed, trying to convince herself as much as Sage.

"No," Sage said sadly. "While you were talking to the police, I texted Reed and Trevor to get out here as fast as possible. I just wanted Trevor to come help you at the house, but now he's going to know that his brother is dead."

Emily watched as Reed walked over to the police and the medics, who would no doubt be the center of attention at Sutter's Bar that night. Word always traveled fast in Oak Hill. Since Reed worked for the city, he knew a lot of the police and medical personnel, and he seemed to recognize at least one of the officers in the group. After a short while, Reed returned and told Emily and Sage to head back to the house. "But do not," he warned sternly, "say a single word to Trevor about his brother's jacket. The police want to notify the Williams family formally once they know more."

Emily let out a groan. How was she supposed to go down to the house and talk to Trevor as if everything was fine? Things were definitely not fine, and he would know it as soon as he looked at her.

Of course, anyone who had just seen human remains come flying out of the ground would be upset. Trevor wouldn't question her emotional state, but still Emily hated having to hide the truth from him. This was how town gossip started, though. If she told Trevor, he'd tell his dad, and the rumor would spread until the whole town knew that Dillan Williams had never gotten farther out of town than Hilltop Cemetery. As it was, word that something was wrong at the cemetery was probably already spreading like wildfire—there were a few people who always tuned in to the police radio frequencies. No one needed to know any more details for the moment.

Emily and Sage took Nathan and Brianne down with them, saying nothing about Dillan's name on the letterman jacket. Brianne was still crying, but she had calmed down considerably. Emily felt a rush of sympathy for her; the poor girl just wasn't cut out for frightening encounters like she'd had the past few days. Reed stayed in the cemetery, promising to relay any information he learned.

Rather than going up to their room, Nathan and Brianne settled into the parlor with Emily and Sage. The four of them sat there in silence for a while as they all tried to process what had happened. The only sounds were Brianne's occasional sniffles and Emily's deep inhales. She knew Trevor would be there any minute. Sage had handed her phone back to her after sending the texts, and Trevor had replied that he was going to take his dad home from the doctor then head right over.

Emily's hands started to shake when she heard Trevor's key in the front door. Sage caught her eye and gave her a warning look, and Emily nodded curtly. She wasn't going to accidentally let the truth slip.

Trevor came into the parlor and stopped short in the doorway, his gaze taking in everyone's shocked expressions and Emily's clay-stained cheeks. "Something bad happened," he said quietly.

"We found a body in the cemetery." Emily realized how stupid that sounded—of course there were bodies in the cemetery—and added, "But it's not an official burial. It looks like, like…" She stopped speaking. What was she supposed to say? *It looks like someone murdered your brother and buried him in the cemetery* was not an option.

Surprisingly, it was Brianne who came to Emily's aid.

"Somebody wanted to hide a body, so they buried it out there."

Trevor blanched and reached out to brace himself against the doorframe. "Do they know who it is?" His voice was shaking.

He knows. Somehow, he already knows it's Dillan.

"No," Brianne answered.

Thank you for doing the lying for me, Emily thought. Then she realized Brianne was being honest. She and Nathan didn't know there was a name embroidered on the jacket. As far as they were concerned, the identity of the body was still a complete mystery.

A loud knock on the front door made everyone jolt, and Trevor looked nervous as he went to open it. In a moment, two police officers came into the parlor, accompanied by Reed. "We're going to need statements from each of you," one of them said. "Is there a room we can use to speak privately with everyone involved?"

"Of course." Emily stood and pointed toward the dining room. "You can use that room. I'll go put some coffee on."

As Emily stepped into the hallway, Trevor plucked at her sleeve to get her attention. He leaned in and whispered, "Do I need to stay?"

The pity Emily felt for Trevor was so strong it almost hurt physically. She wanted to hug him and tell him that everything was okay, but even that would be untrue. When he found out the truth that he clearly already suspected, she knew he would be devastated. Emily put her hand on Trevor's arm. "No, you go on home. I'm sorry you came all the way out here for nothing."

"Just…" Trevor paused and licked his lips nervously. "Keep me posted, please."

Emily promised, and then Trevor turned and hurried out of the house, not even taking the time to say goodbye.

16

The afternoon felt endless. Emily lost count of the rounds she made with the carafe of coffee, constantly refilling cups. Earlier in the morning, Emily had been drinking coffee to stay awake. Now, she was cradling the warm cup in her hands to combat the chill that had taken hold of her body.

Emily had been the first to give her statement to the police, handing over the necklace with the heart-shaped pendant and explaining its discovery, as well. Then Nathan, Brianne, and finally Sage all had to document their experiences. More police had been dispatched to the cemetery, and Reed had been bouncing between the house and the Clements plot, keeping Emily informed of the intense amount of photographing, measuring, and documenting happening on the hill.

Now, Reed was giving his statement in the dining room. Nathan and Brianne had retreated upstairs to their room, so Emily and Sage were alone in the parlor. Sage had remained unusually quiet. The silence in the room felt heavy, and Emily was anxious for some conversation, but her feeble attempts to engage Sage in smalltalk had yielded only short, one-word answers.

"Sage," Emily said, deciding to be completely direct, "I

understand that you're upset, but you are never this quiet. I'm concerned. What's on your mind?"

"Other than the fact that we found the dead body of a classmate today?" Sage's voice was still slightly pitched, as if she was fighting off a rising hysteria.

Please don't freak out, Emily silently pleaded with her. *I won't be able to deal with it if you freak out.*

Sage set down her coffee cup and gestured broadly with both hands. "There's a lot on my mind. First of all, it never occurred to me that this haunting might involve someone with a connection to us. Second, I knew, Em. The instant I realized it was a letterman jacket, I knew there was a body buried there. I deal with departed souls every day, but they're just that: souls, ghosts, that part of us that exists as energy. Not a physical dead body." Sage paused and blew out a breath. "As it turns out, I don't like dead bodies. At all."

"I prefer them when they're a century old and buried six feet under," Emily said, turning up one corner of her mouth in a smile. The joke fell flat, but Sage at least gave her an appreciative glance.

"I'm also really confused," Sage continued.

"How so?"

"We know that the ghost who's been causing trouble here all week is female. We have the dreams and the necklace to support that idea. Yet here we are with Dillan's body. What are we missing?"

Emily shrugged. "I asked Reed the same thing. They must be connected somehow."

The silence returned as both women sat in thought. Sage had drained her cup, refilled it, and drained it again before she broke the silence. "Let's say they were a couple, Dillan and your ghost. They're out at the cemetery, probably during one of those parties, and they get in a fight. He snatches the necklace from her neck and strangles her in his anger. He was probably drunk, too, since kids came out here for that. But he didn't kill her. Maybe she killed him. Or maybe he tripped and fell, and died accidentally. Either way, she was worried about being blamed, so she buried his body to hide it. Now that she's dead, too, his ghost is haunting her. When she was channeling 'it's him' through the automatic writing, we assumed the victim was afraid of her killer. Maybe the killer is afraid of her victim, who is trying to get revenge in the afterlife."

"Does that theory feel right to you?"

Sage actually put a hand against her stomach, as if she could physically feel her intuition. "Not really," she admitted.

"Maybe the police will find out something with their forensics team, or whoever checks stuff like this out. There didn't seem to be a whole lot left of him, though."

"No. Not surprising. After being buried for, what, more than fifteen years or so in a shallow grave like that, you're not likely to last long."

Emily shivered. That chill just wouldn't go away. "Seventeen years. My grandparents were still running this place then. How did they not realize there was a fresh grave in the cemetery?"

"Because the Clements plot was overgrown for decades," Reed answered from the doorway. Finished with his statement, he came in and dropped down next to Emily. "One of the reasons that brick wall around the plot was in such bad shape is because the area was overgrown with holly bushes for years. I was just telling the police that if someone had wanted to stash a body, they picked a good place. You could dig under a tangle of branches, then cover the body again with dirt, and the branches would fall right back into place. You'd never notice the dirt had been disturbed. I'm just surprised that the previous sexton didn't find the body when they cleared that plot. It was only, oh, seven or eight years ago. I think they just cut the bushes at the base rather than digging up the roots. If they had taken out everything, they would have made the discovery, not you."

"Nathan and Brianne, really," Emily said. "They found what turned out to be the jacket. I'm happy to let them have the credit."

"Yes, but they're just out-of-town visitors. It's you that the town will be gossiping about."

"Great."

Reed leaned sideways until his shoulder touched Emily's. "I know you're worried. Because if this really is the body of Dillan Williams, then that means his murderer might have been someone who went to Oak Hill High, too."

"Yeah." Emily paused as her thoughts continued to take shape. "Yeah! Sage and I were just discussing possibilities, and how our female ghost figures into all of this. We think maybe the ghost was Dillan's girlfriend at the time, and somehow he wound up dead when they were out here together. But there is a chance someone else was involved. Maybe she was seeing someone else and Dillan found out, and he got killed when he fought the other guy. Maybe someone had it out for both of them, and the police will find her body, too. Or maybe—"

"Whoa, Em!" Sage gave a little laugh before turning serious again. "Before you turn this into some kind of true-crime drama, let's remember that oftentimes, the most likely answer is the simplest. If you keep going, you'll wind up implicating our whole class as being members of some murder cult."

"My imagination isn't quite that wild," Emily said defensively.

"We're going to ask our ghost some very specific questions tonight," Sage said in response.

"After the day we've had, you still want to do the séance?"

"Yes, more than ever. Reed, are you staying?"

Reed nodded. "I'm with Sage on this, Emily. I trust the police to do good work, but it might be difficult for them to try to pick up the pieces of such an old murder. If we can go directly to someone who was involved, it might be helpful. And if we get any information, we can pass it along to the police."

"Fine," Emily agreed, holding up her hands in mock surrender. "But as soon as the police are gone, I'm taking a nap."

Emily was true to her word. The afternoon was well advanced by the time everything was done and the house quieted down again. Reed went home, but Sage stretched out on the parlor sofa with an afghan that she found in the hall closet.

It wasn't until Emily was curled up in her bed, lying on her side with the covers tucked in tight around her, that the emotions of the day finally caught up with her. She had gone from shock to a quiet seriousness as she realized that someone had been murdered in the cemetery, but now she was overcome with grief. Someone she had grown up with was dead, buried hastily and without any respect. She and Dillan had never been more than classmates and acquaintances, but Emily was especially sad for his family. She didn't think she would ever be able to get the image of Trevor's expression when she told him about the body out of her mind.

Emily was still crying when she fell asleep, utterly exhausted after everything that had happened.

In her dream, Emily's bedroom was murky, like it was filled with smoke or a thick, brown fog. She was standing in the middle of the room, and Dillan was right in front of her, his blond hair disheveled. Those same skinny arms from the first dream were extended toward him, the hands grasping Dillan's letterman jacket. Dillan jerked back, ripping her hands away with his own. He was glaring as he growled, "Who the hell do you think you are?"

Dillan's image dissolved, and now Emily was standing in front of her mirror, but all she could see of her reflection was a delicate gold necklace draped around her neck and arms that were still reaching out in desperation. She opened her mouth to speak, but the voice that came out didn't sound like hers. It was younger, more breathy, but it was shouting.

"It's me! It's me! It's me!"

17

Emily woke up with the words still on her lips. Her room was still dim, but unlike the dream, it was simply because the sun had gone down and the only illumination came from the last glow of twilight on the horizon. The chill was worse than ever, and Emily went straight to the shower, cranking up the water as hot as she could stand it.

The shower helped clear her head a little bit, but she still felt rattled as she got dressed in jeans and a cozy navy-blue sweater and pulled her hair into a bun. As she gave herself a last look in the mirror, the jewelry box caught Emily's eye. Before she could second-guess herself, she opened it and pulled out a necklace of her own. It was a silver chain instead of gold like the ghost's, and the pendant was a graceful letter *E*. Scott had given it to her for their first anniversary, explaining that the *E* stood for three things: Emily, Eternal Rest, and Every Day I Love You More. Emily usually only wore it for special occasions, when she had a good excuse to dress up, but the soft weight of the pendant felt reassuring. Scott's spirit hadn't made any contact since his death, but wearing the necklace made it feel like a part of him was present.

Sage was fast asleep on the sofa when Emily peeked into the parlor. She quietly shut the door and tiptoed out of the house. It was completely dark now, but Emily had grabbed her flashlight so she could see what was happening at the Clements plot.

As soon as she turned toward the cemetery, the police car parked in the grass told her it was being guarded. She relaxed, knowing that meant she wouldn't see last night's mysterious visitor. There were bright lights up on the hill, and as she got closer Emily could see that the police had set up a couple of portable spotlights. She could hear the hum of a generator nearby.

Two men in thick black jackets were leaning against the wall of a nearby mausoleum as Emily approached the Clements plot. In the glow of her flashlight, she saw them stiffen at her approach. "Hi, it's just me!" she called. "Emily from Eternal Rest."

The men relaxed, and as she approached them, Emily could see the Oak Hill Police logo on their jackets. They introduced themselves as Roger and Miles. "I just wanted to come check on things out here," Emily explained, feeling like that was a lame excuse.

"I can't blame you for being curious," said the taller one, Miles. "This place is going to be under watch through tomorrow, at least. They got most of the work done today, but they don't think they've extracted everything yet."

"Everything? You mean, as in all the bones?"

Roger was nodding. "And some clothing. Clothes last a lot longer than skin and organs do."

"Do you know who the victim was?" Emily hoped her tone sounded innocent.

"We're still investigating," Miles said firmly.

Emily looked over at the spot where the body had been buried. The jacket and all of the bones that had scattered when Nathan pulled it out of the ground had been removed, and there was a small pile of dirt on the path that had grown up as the search continued for the rest of the remains.

The lights were so bright that everything beyond them was just black, and Emily thought again of the form she had seen walking toward them the night before. Soon she found herself explaining to Roger and Miles that they should be on the lookout for the man, emphasizing Reed's encounter with him, too. Emily still wasn't convinced that what she had seen had been a living human, but Reed had definitely seen a real man.

After making a promise to return with hot coffee, Emily headed back to the house. She was disappointed not to have learned anything new, but she felt safer knowing the cemetery was being guarded.

Sage was just opening the parlor door as Emily walked in the house. "Any news?" Sage yawned.

"No news. However, I'm making coffee for the officers up at the plot, so come on back and I'll make some for you, too." *Emily Buchanan, Coffee Maker Extraordinaire*, she thought wryly.

Unlike Emily, Sage had slept soundly, with no dreams that she could remember. She took great interest in Emily's dream, but she couldn't come up with a definitive explanation for the ghost's words, either.

"I swear," said Sage, "that someday I'm going to start offering effective communication courses for spirits. I'll invite them all to a séance and then just lecture them about being clear and to the point."

Nathan and Brianne came downstairs eventually, and Emily offered to make a big pot of spaghetti for everyone. They, like Sage, had both slept soundly all afternoon. As they all sat down at the dining room table to eat, Sage laid out her plans for the séance.

Brianne started shifting uncomfortably in her chair, and as Sage continued talking, she put down her fork and pushed her bowl away.

"Brianne?" Emily gave her a sympathetic look. "You don't have to participate if you don't want to."

Brianne looked anxiously at Nathan. "I don't want to," she said quietly.

Nathan reached over and took her hand. "I think that's a good idea. You've had enough scares for one weekend."

Emily wished fleetingly that she could back out of the séance, too, then realized she really didn't want to. She wanted answers, and this might be their best shot at learning anything new.

"If you don't want to be upstairs by yourself, you can wait for us in the parlor," Emily suggested. "We'll be right across the hall."

"Thanks." Brianne gave a relieved smile and returned to her spaghetti.

"So that's four of us for tonight," Sage said. "Reed will be here in about half an hour. We'll get started once he arrives."

There were footsteps on the porch as Sage spoke, but there were too many for it to be just Reed. It was the four women, and Emily realized she had forgotten all about her other guests amid everything else going on. They trooped into the house, talking loudly and excitedly. One of them looked into the dining room. "In here!" she shouted.

Soon they were all sitting or standing around the table, giving a rundown of the stores they had visited, the things they had bought, and what they had eaten for lunch and dinner. Finally, one of them hushed the others and said, "So, what's with the cop car?"

Emily exchanged a look with Sage and steeled herself. "I have some unfortunate news," she began. Quickly, giving as few details as possible, Emily told them about their discovery in the cemetery. Instead of being horrified, the women seemed rather excited.

"I mean, it's awful, of course," one of them said. "A

130

murder victim! But it's like something you'd see on a TV show, isn't it?"

The others agreed heartily and gushed over their good luck in booking rooms at Eternal Rest on such a fortuitous weekend. Emily was slightly horrified they weren't more shocked, but also relieved they weren't upset. She had never had a week in which she worried so much about guests running out of the house screaming or demanding refunds. Or leaving bad reviews. The way these ladies were talking, she wasn't sure she wanted any of them leaving online reviews, even if they were positive ones. She could just picture it: *Five stars! Real dead bodies and a ghost that will chuck all your clothes out the window!*

Eventually, the ladies calmed down enough to tell Emily that they had only returned to Eternal Rest to drop off the things they had bought and change clothes. They were heading back to the bar. Brianne's face visibly perked up at that news, and soon she was a part of the plan, too.

Good. She needs a break from all of this, and she'll have a good time with this bunch. Plus, we'll have a quiet, empty house for the séance.

Reed arrived just as the women were all heading out the door, and he walked into the dining room looking slightly ruffled. He smoothed his gray sweater and patted his hair carefully. "Better warn all the guys who are at Sutter's right now," he mumbled. "I feel like I've been hit by a tornado."

Emily had only just said hello when Sage clapped her hands together. "Right, let's get started! I don't want to waste any time."

Emily was already in her usual spot, closest to the door and the light switch. Once again, Sage sat to her right and Reed took a seat opposite her. Nathan had brought his tape recorder, and he placed it on the table near Sage's séance instruments, explaining that if the ghost was again too shy to communicate with all of them, maybe she would at least say something in the form of an EVP again.

As before, Emily turned off the lights so that only the candle illuminated the room. Sage asked Reed to say a prayer for protection, and then she clearly explained which ghost they wanted to communicate with and how the ghost could do it.

Then Sage dove right in with, "We found the body today. Did you kill him?"

Silence.

"Maybe," Emily said quietly, "we should take a slightly less accusatory approach. If I was a ghost and a psychic medium asked me a question like that, I'd keep my mouth shut, too."

Sage reluctantly agreed and asked instead, "Were you with him when he died out in the cemetery?"

Still nothing.

For forty-five minutes, Sage asked questions and no one answered. She even requested that Mrs. Thompson or one of the other Eternal Rest ghosts come forward, but there was no answer. Emily could see Sage shaking her head in frustration, her face looking pinched in the light of the candle. "I don't understand," she said. "This house feels empty. It has never felt that way before. I noticed the spiritual silence earlier, but then I was purposely trying to keep myself psychically closed off so I could conserve my energy. I thought it was just me who wasn't receiving, but it's like they're all gone."

"It was Emily who got the ghost to talk to us during the EVP session on Friday," Nathan suggested. "Maybe she can try?"

Sage gestured toward Emily. "Have at it."

Emily cleared her throat as she thought carefully about what to say. She thought of her dream, and she reached her hand up to wrap her fingers around her necklace. "You came to me in my dream again," Emily began. "You said 'it's me,' but I don't know what that means. Can you tell us?"

Again, silence.

Emily tried asking a few other questions, but Sage continued to report feeling a sort of spiritual void in the house. Even Emily could tell the atmosphere didn't have the same feeling that it often did when paranormal activity was happening. On the nights that Sage got a lot of responses from the ghosts, like knocking noises and channeled messages, there was a sort of buzz in the air, as if it were electrified. Earlier in the week, the atmosphere had felt heavy. Now, it just felt completely normal.

When they had been sitting there for more than an hour, Sage threw up her hands and said in an annoyed tone, "Okay, we're done. Emily, get the lights."

Emily complied as Sage blew out the candle. They sat there for a few minutes, sharing theories about what had possibly happened to the ghosts, when the atmosphere did begin to change. Sage noticed it first, but soon even Emily could feel it. It was different than anything she had felt before. Even though they were just sitting around the table, she suddenly felt anxious. She began to breathe heavier, and she started looking warily over her shoulder toward the closed door.

"What's happening?" Emily asked.

Sage had her eyes closed in concentration. Nathan and Reed looked as uncomfortable as Emily felt, and all three of them turned their eyes to the psychic medium, hoping for an answer. Sage's head moved slowly from side to side, as if she were searching for something. "I feel fear, dread, the desire to run away," she said, the words rolling together. "I'm anxious, I don't want to be found, I don't want him to see me, I don't want him to find me, I don't want him to touch me…"

A soft sound from the surface of the table drew everyone's eyes downward. The pencil for automatic writing was slowly rolling toward Sage. Emily grabbed the paper and pushed it in front of Sage. "Write!" Emily said anxiously.

Sage picked up the pencil and started to write. This time, though, she wrote just one single message, right in the middle of the page: *He's here!*

18

Sage's hand banged the pencil onto the paper to make the dot on the exclamation point, and the lead broke with a sharp snap. At the same time, the doorbell rang and Emily, already feeling anxious from the strange energy pervading the room, jumped. She rose, shaking, and Reed quickly got up and walked in front of her to the door. "I'm going with you," he said firmly.

Reed opened the door cautiously at first, then let out a breath and opened it wide, revealing a stocky man with close-cropped blond hair that was graying at the temples. It was Roger, one of the police officers guarding the cemetery. Roger was frowning, his eyes constantly shifting toward the cemetery, and the brief bit of relief Emily had felt when she saw him disappeared.

"Miss Emily, do you have any guests who might be wandering the cemetery tonight?" he asked.

"No. One of our guests is in here, with us. The others are in town tonight." Emily knew what was coming next, and her shoulders tensed.

"Then I think that mysterious man you told us about is back. Miles had walked down to the squad car for his scarf, and when he came back, he clearly saw someone walking along the path that leads to the Clements plot. He thought he spied a second person, as well, but it was too dark to really tell."

"He's here." It was Sage's voice. She and Nathan had come out into the hallway, too. "That's what the ghost meant. He's here, not in the house, but in the cemetery."

Emily stepped past Roger and walked to the left side of the porch, peering out toward the cemetery as if she might actually see something. The lights at the Clements plot sent up a bright beacon, illuminating the lower branches of an oak tree above them, but otherwise everything was dark.

Emily turned to face Roger. "Could Miles see any features?"

"No, ma'am." Emily bristled at the term but held back from remarking that she was probably fifteen years younger than Roger and still too young for that title. "Miles saw a man walking, and he seemed to be dressed all in black. There was some movement slightly behind him, but it could have been just shadows, and not actually another person. Miles was doing a sweep with his flashlight, and when he brought the light back to the spot, the man was gone. He probably dove off the path to hide, but Miles wasn't able to find him again."

"If there was anybody to find," Nathan said quietly. He turned to Sage. "Could it have been a ghost?"

Sage shrugged slowly, but Emily recognized the far-away look in her eyes as she still sought to feel some sort of presence. "They're coming back. The ghosts. I think we didn't feel them in the house because they were in the cemetery, doing their own watch. If they're coming back, the man must be gone, whether he's living or just a spirit."

Roger gave a loud cough, as if to remind them that he was still there. "I don't know about this ghost stuff. No offense, Miss Emily. I know that's what brings people to your place, but Miles definitely saw someone. An actual person. We'll keep a sharp eye out for him in case he turns up again."

"He won't," Sage said confidently. "Not tonight, at least."

Roger was looking at her out of the corner of his eye, one brow raised skeptically. Emily quickly intervened. "Thank you so much for letting us know. I really can't express how much I appreciate you being out here tonight, after everything that happened today."

Roger smiled, and on impulse, Emily pulled her keyring out of her pocket and worked the key to the back door off of it, presenting it to Roger like a gift. "There's a bathroom off the hallway, and the coffee maker in the kitchen is pretty easy to figure out. I'll leave a few of the baked goods out, too. Help yourself. The back door sticks sometimes, especially after rain, so just give it an extra nudge if you need to."

Now Roger was positively beaming. He thanked Emily profusely, gave Sage another doubtful look, and returned to the cemetery, promising to return the key in the morning.

"Unbelievers," Sage said dramatically as soon as Roger was out of earshot, but the corners of her mouth were turned up in amusement. She knew that a lot of Oak Hill residents thought she was a fraud or, worse, some kind of hellish abomination, but Sage had always accepted it with humor.

"The ghost just gave us a real-time warning of the man in the cemetery," Nathan was saying. "That's amazing!"

Emily had to agree, but that still didn't tell them who the man was or why he was stalking around the cemetery. If it was Dillan's ghost, then why was he still out there? His body had been found, so why would his spirit still be lurking around? Was he still trying to get revenge on his killer?

Before Emily could open her mouth to articulate any of these thoughts, Sage said quietly, "They're tired."

Of course the ghosts would be exhausted after their watch in the cemetery. One look at everyone, and it was clear to Emily that even the living were exhausted, too.

Emily heard the rest of her guests return well before midnight. She had already turned off her light but was still awake, and it felt good to know the house was full once again. The one couple barely made a sound as they ascended the stairs, and the hushed but happy voices of the women returning from Sutter's was a nice little burst of positivity to end what had been a long, strange day.

On Sunday morning, Emily had just gotten dressed when she heard the back door open. Roger and Miles were heading home after an all-night vigil, and they reported that it had been quiet during their shift. Sage's hunch had been right. Emily had awoken twice during the night when she heard one of the officers come in, and she was pleased to see they had taken advantage of the baked goods she had left out for them.

Emily had expected a quiet morning, but her doorbell rang right as her first guests were making their way to the dining room. When she opened the door, Emily was surprised to see the preacher from Oak Hill Baptist Church. "I just wanted to stop by on my way to morning services," he said gently, "to extend my sympathy for your situation."

Emily blinked in confusion. "My situation?"

"We heard they found a body yesterday, out in the cemetery."

"Yes, they did. Thank you for stopping by."

After a few more pleasantries, and the promise that the

entire congregation would pray for the deceased that morning, the preacher departed. As Emily watched his car pull out of the driveway and onto the road, another car was turning in. She instantly recognized Trish's car.

Trish leapt out of her car after she put it in park, leaving the engine running. "I can't stay long," she said, rushing up the steps to give Emily a brief hug. "I heard about the body. Oh my God, can you believe it? I wonder who it is, and who killed them. Rumor has it the body was wearing an Oak Hill High letterman jacket."

Emily confirmed the information for Trish, who just shook her head and said again, "I wonder who it is. I mean, there are rumors, of course. The only student who's gone missing in the past few decades is Dillan Williams. Do you think it could be him? That's what some people are saying. Imagine if it is, right after his brother moved back to town! Absolutely crazy. Okay, well, I'm off. I've got to get to the bakery. I'm going to make up some of those Victorian funeral cookies. I bet they'll sell like mad today!"

Trish dashed back to her car and was soon gone, leaving Emily feeling slightly breathless. No matter what time of day she came by, Trish always seemed to be over-flowing with energy.

All of the guests except one of the women, who was apparently a little hungover this morning, were already in the dining room. Emily went in to say good morning and discovered that the couple from Florida had heard about the body the evening before, when someone called a relative of theirs to share the news. There really were no secrets in Oak Hill.

Emily was getting the blow-by-blow report of the ladies' evening at the bar when the doorbell rang again.

"Seriously?" Emily grumbled as she opened the front door. This time, it was someone she didn't even know.

The woman, wearing a pretty floral dress buried under

a thick brown coat, nodded her head briskly. "Good morning. I was wondering if you'd be so kind as to let me leave these at the cemetery gate." The woman held up a bouquet of flowers. "The policeman out front says we can't go inside today."

Emily glanced toward the cemetery and saw the woman was correct. Not only were they keeping the Clements plot secure, but the entire cemetery was now being guarded. Emily nodded and said, "I'm sorry you're not able to go in and visit your ancestor. Which family are you related to?"

"Oh, I don't have anyone buried out here," the woman answered, looking at Emily incredulously. "These flowers are for that poor dead person they found yesterday, of course."

"Of course." Emily tried to give her most understanding smile.

"You take care, my dear," the woman said, reaching out to squeeze Emily's hand. Then she was off to the cemetery, and Emily watched her lovingly prop the bouquet next to the front gate.

Shaking her head, Emily went back inside.

A few more people showed up during the next hour, most heading straight to the cemetery. Emily walked out to find that several more bouquets had been added, and someone had even left a white seven-day candle.

As more and more people from Oak Hill began to arrive to pay their respects, Emily's guests slowly began to talk about finishing their packing and checking out. They were clearly reluctant to go, and Emily knew they wanted to stick around as long as possible to see the spectacle.

Finally, though, just before lunch, the group of ladies left, making as much noise on their way out as they had on their arrival. They were already making plans to come back at the same time the next year. The couple had checked out shortly before them, heading to one last lunch with their family before driving home.

Nathan and Brianne were sitting on the front porch, wrapped up in light jackets and watching cars continue to stream into the driveway since the cemetery parking spots were all full. At the moment, there was a short line of people waiting to put down their offerings or simply stand respectfully in front of the cemetery gate. Judging by the number of people in nice outfits, Emily assumed most of them had come straight from church to the cemetery. Oak Hill's congregations must have been buzzing with the news.

Emily walked onto the porch and leaned against one of the columns as she pulled her gold-hued cardigan tight around her body and crossed her arms. She watched the people coming and going from the gate, relieved the police had blocked the cemetery. Otherwise, who knew what kind of trampled mess the influx of visitors might leave behind.

"We need to hit the road soon," Nathan said sadly. "Will you be all right?"

"Yeah. I've got Sage and Reed to look after me." Emily smiled genuinely at the couple. "You two have been really amazing. Thank you so much for all of your help and for putting up with this mess."

Brianne nonchalantly waved a hand. She looked well-rested, and Emily suspected that getting out of the house and away from paranormal activity for a night had been just what she needed. "We wanted to go looking for ghosts on this trip," she said. "We just didn't know they'd come looking for us!"

"But finding a dead body wasn't on your itinerary. The next time you want to come here for a weekend, it's on me. And I promise that next time, there won't be any dead bodies!"

Nathan and Brianne thanked Emily profusely and

promised to come back, hinting that they might just coordinate their dates with the women who had taken Brianne under their wing.

By one o'clock, Emily once again had Eternal Rest to herself, if she didn't count the visitors still arriving at the cemetery. Every so often, someone she knew would come up to the house to see how she was doing, so getting the rooms cleaned and ready for the next round of guests took much longer than usual. Emily realized there wouldn't even be time for a Sunday afternoon nap.

By nightfall, the impromptu memorial had grown to an enormous size, making Emily wonder if everyone in Oak Hill had been there. Hastily-made signs had even been hung on the gate, with messages like *never forgotten* and *in our hearts*. Emily found it all to be a little much, considering none of those people even knew the identity of the body.

That night, Emily dreamed she was in the cemetery, looking toward the house from the Clements plot. The porch light shone in the distance, the only illumination other than the stars. A form was moving up the walkway, stalking toward her. She tried to run, but her feet refused to cooperate. She stood there watching as the form got closer, looking bigger and more menacing with every step. It was shrouded in shadow, but Emily felt like it was someone she knew. Despite the sense of familiarity, she also felt a rising fear. She put out her hands as the form got closer, but her fingers went right through his chest, as if he were made of smoke.

The form took another step closer, and dimly, Emily could see its face now, twisted with emotion.

Emily woke up with a shriek. It was Trevor's face that had been staring at her.

Emily didn't sleep for the rest of the night. She couldn't decide if the dream had been yet another message from the ghost or her own mind, reliving the look she had seen on Trevor's face when she had told him about the discovery of the body. Emily realized she hadn't checked on Trevor to see how he was doing. She should have, she knew, but she had been hesitant to contact him, afraid she would let slip her own conviction that the body was Dillan's.

And if the dream had been a message from the ghost, then that didn't make Emily feel any better. In the pre-dawn hours, Emily sat in the parlor wrapped in a blanket. She hadn't turned the page of her book for twenty minutes as she considered for the first time that maybe Trevor knew something about all of this.

Or, worse, maybe Trevor had actually had some part in the murder.

Emily's idea of a love triangle came back into her mind, and she tried to push it away. *No*, she told herself firmly, *I am not going to suspect my own employee. That's ridiculous.*

Emily had more guests coming in, a rare Monday through Thursday stay for a family. Ordinarily she would remain home in case they arrived early, but she felt the overwhelming urge to get out of the house.

She saw Reed pulling up at the cemetery as she was locking the front door. Emily walked over, watching him gesture to the police officer currently on gate-guarding duty. Reed was shaking his head as Emily reached him, and he turned when he heard her step on the grass.

"I can't get into my own cemetery," Reed said, clearly annoyed. "My team and I need to clean up after that storm on Friday."

"I've had enough of the cemetery for the time being." It was the first time Emily could remember ever feeling like that, and she didn't like it. Hilltop Cemetery was as much her home as Eternal Rest, but right now it just didn't feel that way. She smiled politely at the police officer as she linked her arm through Reed's, guiding him toward his car so they wouldn't be overheard. "I had a dream last night," she said in a low voice.

"I think Sage was right," Reed said after Emily had described seeing Trevor's face. His voice was gentle, but Emily could also detect a slightly amused tone. "You want to turn this into a drama. This isn't TV. When Trevor heard the news, he acted like someone who was shocked and sad, not someone who was guilty."

"You're right," Emily conceded. "I'm frustrated and stressed and confused. My brain is probably communicating as badly as this ghost."

"I'm going to call my team and tell them to head to the Garden," Reed said, referring to the modern cemetery. "We'll work there until Hilltop is open again. Are you going to be okay out here by yourself?"

"I'm heading out, too, but I'll call you if anything else happens."

Emily was sitting in her car before it occurred to her that she didn't even know where she was going. "Get out of the house" had been her only thought. It was too early to get lunch at the café, and Sage wouldn't open her shop until ten.

Instead, Emily drove to the library. She told herself she would check out a couple of books, maybe some fantasy novels that would transport her as far away from reality as possible.

Her feet seemed to know where they were going before she did, walking toward the records room. Soon, Emily had a stack of microfiche files of *The Oak Hill Monitor* from early in her senior year. She remembered that Dillan had gone missing just after homecoming, but before Halloween. Eventually she found what she was looking for. The newspaper dated October third of that year had a headline reading "Local Teen Missing: Search Underway."

The article didn't really help. It mentioned that Dillan had been the star of the homecoming football game two weeks before his disappearance, and it mentioned a volunteer group of locals who were going to search all the side roads and forested areas around Oak Hill.

It was the article dated one week later that really got Emily's attention. She was surprised to see her own grandfather quoted.

"We know the teenagers in Oak Hill like coming to the cemetery at night," said Leon Buchanan, who owns the land on which Hilltop Cemetery is built. "A few of us got together and looked all over the woods behind the cemetery, but we didn't find any sign of Dillan Williams. All we found was a pile of beer cans."

Emily chuckled, picturing the sour expression she knew her grandfather had on his face when he made that statement to the reporter. He had always kept a trash bag tucked in his back pocket when he went to the cemetery, and he would always come home muttering about litterbugs. The articles hadn't given Emily any more insight into how the body wound up in Hilltop Cemetery, but it had been nice reading her grandfather's words. It felt like he was reaching out to her.

The final article, dated more than a month after the first one, was just one paragraph long. It said that Dillan was still missing and that after extensive interviews, the police had run out of any leads pertaining to his where-abouts. *Such a sad ending.* Emily's heart went out to Mr. Williams, who must have been devastated to lose his eldest son. And not just to lose him, but to have no knowledge of whether or not he was still alive.

Emily wondered what gossip had reached his ears about the body.

A quick glance at the clock on the wall told Emily she was running out of time to get back to Eternal Rest before that day's guests arrived. She had planned to swing by Sage's shop to fill her in on everything, but on impulse, she decided to visit Trevor instead. A text or a phone call would have been more comfortable for her, but after every-thing he had been through the past week, Emily felt like a visit was the proper thing to do.

Emily hadn't used a phone book in an age, but the library had one, and soon she was on her way to Manor Hills, an older but still swank housing development in Oak Hill. The houses there made Eternal Rest look modest in size. Some of them had been well-maintained, while others had a sort of faded gentility to them.

The Williams house was in that latter category. Its two-story facade was brick, with a wide porch fronted by a white railing. The bricks looked like they could use a thor-ough pressure-washing, and the paint was in need of a touch-up. Still, the lawn and front flower beds were neatly trimmed, and it was obvious that Mr. Williams took a lot of pride in his house.

Emily took a deep breath and let it out slowly before ringing the front doorbell. It was Mr. Williams who answered, and he looked pleased to see her. "Good morning, Emily. What a nice surprise. Please, come in," he said warmly, standing back and gesturing her into a spacious living room.

"Good morning, Mr. Williams. I'm sorry about dropping by unannounced. I was hoping I could catch up with Trevor."

"Of course, of course. Ah, here he is." Trevor was hurrying down the stairs, taking them two at a time. Mr. Williams winked at Emily. "Wish I could still move that fast."

"Good morning!" Trevor said brightly. "I was going to go out for a run, but maybe we can walk together?"

"Sure." Emily tried to match Trevor's bright tone, even though it was startling.

Mr. Williams moved slowly to a big recliner in front of the TV, so Emily turned her attention to a wall full of photographs as she waited for Trevor to put on his shoes. There was a school photo of Dillan, and Emily easily remembered his carefully-styled dark-blond hair and green eyes. Between his looks and his outgoing personality, he had been popular at school. Judging by the family photos, Dillan had taken after their mother, whom Emily had never met. Emily could especially see the resemblance in the old wedding photo of Mr. and Mrs. Williams. *What a difference the decades and cancer have made*, Emily thought sadly. The strong, confident, smiling man in the photo looked so different from the old man who seemed entirely too small to be sitting in such a big recliner.

Soon Trevor was leading the way out the door, and Emily called a farewell to his dad. Outside, Trevor didn't say a word until they had reached the sidewalk. "My dad doesn't know," he said quietly, as if he feared being overheard. His upbeat tone had vanished.

"About the body?"

"Yeah. His last doctor's appointment was on Friday, and he wasn't feeling great this weekend, so he didn't go out at all. I know the whole town is talking about it, but so far I've been able to keep him safe."

Emily stopped and faced Trevor, her hand on his arm. "Trevor…"

"I know it might seem overprotective, but my dad doesn't know what happened to my brother. I don't want him to think that was Dillan who you found in the cemetery."

But it is him, and you know it. You knew it as soon as I told you we'd found a body.

She wanted to say that to Trevor's face, but if he was now choosing to pretend it wasn't Dillan's body they had found, then she wasn't going to intervene. Maybe it was a coping mechanism to help him absorb the shock. Or maybe Trevor really had been involved in one or even both of the murders, as Emily's dream suggested, and he wanted to avoid the subject entirely.

"I understand," she said eventually. And she did understand wanting to protect Mr. Williams. He had enough to deal with already. "I came to see you because I felt bad about Saturday. I'm sorry you had to walk into such a mess. It was kind of Sage to ask you to come help, but obviously not necessary."

Trevor shrugged. "It's okay."

Emily wanted to say more, but Trevor was obviously intent on leaving Dillan out of the discussion. Instead, he turned the subject to how many guests he'd find at Eternal Rest when he arrived on Tuesday.

"We've got a party of six coming in. They arrive today." Emily glanced down at her watch and swore. "I have to go! It's almost noon!"

💀

148

Emily made it back to Eternal Rest before her guests arrived by only ten minutes. Check-in might be two o'clock, but a lot of guests seemed eager to start their stays early. The group was a mini family reunion comprised of one couple with their adult son and daughter, plus their spouses. The grandkids were on Spring Break and attending a week-long camp, which meant the adults could have their own version of camp, too. That was exactly how Mr. Morgan, the patriarch of the family, described it, adding, "But our camp has real beds, showers, and toilets!"

The best kind of camping was the bed and breakfast kind, Emily agreed, and she found herself still smiling as the family headed upstairs to settle into their rooms. Room three was the only one empty, in part because Emily still needed a hand getting the window screen back into place. Trevor would be far more useful than Mrs. Thompson had been when it came to tasks like that: Emily had no qualms about asking Trevor to climb up on a tall ladder.

Monday afternoon passed like so many other days did. With her guests out exploring Oak Hill, Emily had the place to herself to do a few chores, check messages, and fulfill booking requests. It felt like a completely normal day. The only unusual thing was that the police were still guarding the cemetery gate, though later in the afternoon one of them came down to the house to tell Emily they had completed their investigation at the burial site. Her cemetery was open again.

Not able to contain her curiosity, Emily walked up to the Clements plot. The day was sunny, and although it wasn't warm, there wasn't a chill in the air, either. It felt good, and Emily had a lightness in her step that hadn't been there since the morning Rhonda reported her dream. Had it really been only a week since the ring went missing? So much had happened since then.

The area in front of the Clements plot had been thoroughly excavated. The police had filled in the hole they had dug during their search for the rest of the body, but the freshly turned earth made it obvious what a wide area they had been searching. Emily hoped they had recovered all the bones, because she didn't want any visitors to make a surprise discovery.

Reed would be happy to have access to the cemetery again, and she would ask him and his team to make sprucing up the area their first order of business. Even before they rebuilt the brick wall, Emily wanted them to do everything possible to remove all signs of what had happened there.

As the day wore on, things continued feeling back to normal. Trish came by with all of the baked goods for Tuesday morning's breakfast, the guests returned after an early dinner in town, and absolutely nothing paranormal happened.

Emily felt a little nervous going to bed that night, because the normalcy actually felt abnormal. After so much paranormal activity and such a tenacious ghost, it was odd that nothing at all had happened that day.

Despite her apprehension, it was a quiet night at Eternal Rest. Emily woke up a few times, as usual, but there were no strange dreams to rip her out of a peaceful slumber. When she said good morning to the Morgan family in the dining room on Tuesday morning, they all raved about what a good night's sleep they had gotten, and how nice and quiet it was "out here in the country."

Relieved, Emily decided not to worry about the ghost. Maybe things would be quieter again, especially now that the body had been found.

Trevor arrived at nine, and Emily directed him to the ladder stored in a small lean-to addition on one side of the barn. Reinstalling the screen in room three was a two-person job, so Trevor got the ladder in place to bring the screen up as Emily waited inside the room to secure the screen with the little hooks that fastened it to the window frame.

Everything went smoothly, and Emily was latching the last hook when she saw movement in her peripheral vision. She heard Trevor swear loudly and looked up just in time to see him rocking backward.

Lightning-fast, Trevor reached out and grabbed the decorative molding above the window. It wasn't much of a handhold, but it was enough to help him regain his balance. Emily stood there, stunned, her heart beating fast as she realized just how close Trevor had come to falling off the ladder.

Trevor didn't say a word or so much as glance at Emily. As soon as he was balanced again, he began racing down the ladder as if his life depended on it.

Emily ran downstairs and out the front door. By the time she rounded the corner of the house, Trevor was already off the ladder, standing bent over, his hands on his knees.

"Are you okay?" Emily was having to ask Trevor that question entirely too often.

Trevor just nodded, his gaze still fixed on the ground below him as he focused on catching his breath. "I was pushed." He stood up and his eyes met Emily's. She involuntarily took a step back when she saw the anger there. She had expected Trevor to be scared, like her, but not angry.

It wasn't Emily whom Trevor was angry with. His voice was shaking with rage and adrenaline when he spoke again. "That damn ghost just tried to kill me."

20

Emily's arms were half-outstretched, as if she was going to put them around Trevor, but they had frozen in place. "What?" She could hear the disbelief in her own voice.

"I felt something, like pressure against my chest," Trevor explained. "And it just pushed me backwards. If I hadn't caught myself…"

Emily nodded, her eyes turning to the top of the ladder. Trevor didn't need to finish his sentence. He had narrowly avoided falling, and even if the two-story drop hadn't killed him, he would have been severely injured.

"Let's get you inside," Emily said, forcing herself to speak calmly. Emily started to lead the way, but Trevor passed her, his anger powering his stride. He went into the kitchen and sat down heavily in a chair, bracing his elbows on top of the table so he could cradle his head in his hands. He was still breathing hard.

Emily poured a glass of water and put it down in front of Trevor.

"Did you hear anything? See anything?"

"No. I just felt it. I think it was her hand on my chest." Trevor raised his head as his anger ebbed. "Do you think I'm crazy?"

"Of course not." Emily sat down opposite him and drummed her fingers anxiously against her thigh. "I'm just surprised. There was zero paranormal activity yesterday. Zero. And then ten minutes after you arrive, you're nearly killed."

"I don't understand what this ghost has against me. First the microwave, and now this."

"I'm still not sure the microwave incident was intended to hurt you. Pushing you off of a ladder, though, is not an accident." Emily paused and thought about Trevor's words again. "You said you think her hand was against your chest. What makes you say that?"

"I felt the pressure there."

"Did it feel like an actual hand?"

Trevor sat up and put a hand against his chest. "No," he said slowly. "It was bigger than that. More like one big something pushing against me."

"An energetic force, then, but not necessarily taking a specific physical form."

Trevor laughed dryly. "Don't you sound like the ghost expert."

"Far from it. However, you and I are both assuming it was the ghost of the woman who's been causing all the problems this past week. Maybe there's somebody else here, too."

Maybe your brother is here.

"It's possible."

Emily started at Trevor's answer, worried for a moment that she had spoken out loud, before she realized he was responding to her suggestion that it was another ghost. "Whoever it is," she said, "it doesn't change the fact that I think you might be in danger as long as you're here. I hate to say it, but you should probably go home."

Trevor was shaking his head, and anger flashed across his face again. "No, I'm not leaving. I'm not going to climb any more ladders today, but I am not going to let this ghost scare me off."

"I'm not going to let you go up any stairs, either!"

A quiet voice called from the hallway, and both Emily and Trevor jumped. "Hello?" Emily called.

It was Mrs. Morgan. Emily and Trevor had been so focused on their discussion that neither one of them had heard her come down the hallway from the dining room. She walked cautiously into the kitchen. "Is everything okay? We heard a shout, and then you came flying down the stairs, Emily."

Emily exchanged a look with Trevor before he answered, "I had a little fight with the ladder, but I won in the end." He smiled reassuringly at Mrs. Morgan.

"I'm glad no one was hurt. Well, we're off to do some sightseeing. You two be safe!"

Emily laughed. If only Mrs. Morgan knew how apt her warning really was.

Emily was afraid to let Trevor out of her sight for the rest of the day. Originally, she had intended to head into town to pick up a few things—the house was dangerously low on toilet paper—but the thought of driving off and leaving Trevor alone in the house made her feel too anxious. Eventually, Emily was able to talk Trevor into making the trip for her, even though he protested that it was giving the ghost what it wanted.

Only one more incident occurred, and it came shortly after Trevor had returned from town. He and Emily brought in the shopping bags and placed them on the dining room table. Emily ran upstairs with the toilet paper rolls while Trevor took some coffee and breakfast supplies into the kitchen. When Emily came back downstairs, she was relieved to find Trevor just finishing up. None of her appliances had attacked him.

When they walked into the dining room, though, they found the rest of the shopping bags pushed onto the floor. A bag of toffee candies, which Emily liked to keep in a cut-glass dish on the parlor coffee table, had been ripped open. The candies had been arranged across the table, spelling out in large letters one word: *HIM.*

21

"Why do I feel like this ghost is singling me out?" Trevor was pacing back and forth on the front porch while Emily sat in the swing, watching him warily. The ghost was singling him out, and she didn't like the suspicious thoughts going through her head. She tried to tell herself that it was because Trevor was Dillan's brother, and maybe the ghost was trying to get a message to him. If that was the case, though, then why had it tried to push him off a ladder? Maybe this was a different ghost than that of the woman, as Emily had speculated. Maybe this was Dillan's ghost. It could even be the spirit of the person who had killed Dillan, and now it was trying to kill Trevor, as well. Emily began thinking about family vendettas and who in Oak Hill might have hated the Williams family enough to start killing them so many years ago.

Emily pinched the ridge between her eyes. "Not a TV show," she mumbled.

"What?"

"Nothing. It's just something Reed said. My brain keeps trying to form dramatic and overly-complicated theories."

Trevor stopped pacing and faced Emily, his hands balled into fists. "Listen," he said tersely, "I know what you think. But, I swear, I have nothing to do with any of this. I have no idea why this ghost seems to be targeting me."

He sounded earnest, and Emily wanted to believe him. She heard Sage in her mind, asking her what her intuition thought. At the moment, though, Emily's intuition was giving her the silent treatment.

Trevor and Emily both looked up at the sound of a car turning into the driveway. Expecting to see her guests returning, Emily was surprised to recognize an Oak Hill Police Department car. The man who stepped out of it was Roger. His face looked grim and sad, and Emily's greeting to him died on her lips.

"Miss Emily." He nodded at her, then looked questioningly at Trevor. Emily introduced him, and Roger gave him a tight smile. "Benjamin's boy, sure. My brother worked for your daddy for years."

Roger turned his attention back to Emily, his smile gone. "May I speak to you in private?"

Emily led Roger into the kitchen, as far from Trevor's renewed pacing as possible, and shut the door. "I just came out here to give you some news about that body," he said, waving off Emily's offer to sit. "Your friend had said she got a look at the name on the jacket, but it's not the Williams boy who was buried there. It's actually a woman. A young woman, from the looks of it."

"Oh." It was all Emily could get out. Her mind was instantly flooded with thoughts, but the one that was fighting the hardest for attention was the memory of her dream from Saturday night. The way her mouth had said the words "it's me." The ghost had been trying to tell Emily that it wasn't Dillan buried there at the Clements plot, but her.

A chill washed over Emily's body as she reframed Dillan's role in this. Emily leaned toward Roger and asked quietly, "What are we supposed to tell Trevor? He doesn't know that the body was wearing Dillan's jacket." Roger looked sad, resolute. "He and his father need to know, and we'll be talking to both of them, of course."

Emily had felt awful talking to Trevor, all while knowing his brother's body had been found. She wasn't at all relieved to have been wrong. Somehow, this felt worse. She had thought telling Trevor his brother was dead would be heartbreaking, but telling him his brother might be a murderer would be even worse. Unless, of course, Trevor already knew who had murdered the woman.

Roger and Emily called Trevor inside and sat down with him in the parlor. Trevor watched them warily and actually shrank back against his chair, as if he were trying to escape whatever they were about to say. Emily let Roger do the talking, knowing he had experience imparting this sort of bad news. As he spoke calmly and plainly, but not unkindly, to Trevor, Emily watched Trevor closely. His hands had a tight grip on the arms on the chair, and his lips were pinched together in a thin line. He kept his eyes fixed on Roger, and his expression never changed when Roger mentioned Dillan's jacket. When Roger finished speaking, Trevor continued staring at him, silent.

The pause grew uncomfortable, and finally Roger cleared his throat. "We'll have to tell your father, of course."

"Of course," Trevor said, his voice thick.

"Let's go now. I'll follow you to your house."

"Okay."

Roger stood, and Trevor followed, his movements wooden. As they reached the front door, Emily called to Trevor. "I'm so sorry," she said.

Trevor gave a curt nod and followed Roger onto the porch without a word.

Emily stood and watched until both of their cars had rounded the bend in the road, and then she sat down heavily on the top step of the porch. It felt like all of the strength had been sapped from her legs. Her brain had been churning before, but now it just felt blank. She couldn't begin to imagine what Trevor was feeling right now, or the pain that Mr. Williams was going to feel in just a matter of minutes. She remembered the shock and the pain of finding out about Scott's death, but at least she had never been told that Scott might be a killer.

And if Dillan had killed the woman, then where was he now? Emily vividly recalled the male form she had seen in the cemetery the night of the EVP session. Had that been Dillan? No, surely not, she told herself. Dillan skipped town seventeen years ago, and he's probably got an entirely new life on the other side of the country.

Then again, she thought, Trevor might have had more to do with this than his brother. It was his face she had seen in her dream, not Dillan's.

The jacket was yet another piece of information that added to the confusion. Emily's dreams flashed through her mind. In the first, she had clearly seen the ghost's arms, and she hadn't been wearing a jacket as she was strangled. In the second dream, Dillan had been wearing his own jacket. And yet, the woman had been wearing his letterman jacket when she was buried.

Emily brought her hands up to clutch the sides of her head, as if she could somehow reach in and sort through her thoughts. She tried to think back over the past week's events, but she felt overwhelmed by all of it.

The line of the road suddenly blurred, and Emily realized she was crying. She gave in and dropped her head onto her knees, sobs welling up to drown out all other thought.

Emily felt a gentle hand on her back. The contact was comforting, and her sobs began to subside a little. Then, with a wave of embarrassment, Emily realized her guests must have come back. She had been so upset she had never heard their cars pulling into the driveway. She shakily drew in several deep breaths in an effort to get her crying under control. When she felt like she could hold it together at least a little bit, she raised her head. "I apologize for my state," she began, then stopped suddenly.

The driveway was empty.

Emily whipped her head around, but she was alone on the porch. The feel of the hand was gone.

She had definitely stopped crying now, her surprise surpassing all other emotion. "H-hello?"

Of course there was no answer. Emily didn't know which ghost had been comforting her, but she didn't feel any fear at all. Unlike Trevor's incident on the ladder, this paranormal activity was meant to be calming, not violent.

"Thank you," Emily called. She shifted her whole body around so that she was facing the front door. "We know now that it was a woman's body found in the cemetery, and I'm assuming it's yours. Did Dillan kill you? Is he the one who ripped off your necklace and strangled you? What's your name?"

Emily sighed. She was asking the kinds of questions that Sage would ask during a séance, or that someone like Nathan would ask during an EVP session. While this ghost had gotten good at moving objects—and people, Emily reminded herself grimly—and channeling messages through dreams and automatic writing, Emily didn't get the impression that the ghost had gotten the hang of speaking. That single EVP from the cemetery was all the ghost had said to them so far.

Thinking of Sage made Emily pop up onto her legs.

She still felt exhausted, but at least she knew what to do next.

Emily's words tumbled out as soon as Sage answered the phone.

"Whoa, slow down!" Sage said. "Sit tight, and I'll be right there."

Sage was true to her word, making the drive from her house to Emily's in just over ten minutes. Sage lived on the other side of downtown Oak Hill, and while it was a small town, Emily knew Sage must have broken the speed limit by a hefty amount to make it that quickly.

"You're a mess," Sage said as soon as she saw Emily. She licked her thumb and began to rub off the mascara that had run down onto Emily's cheek.

Emily batted at her hand. "Gross! Stop!"

Sage rubbed her thumb against the side of her black dress, which was covered with bright pink polka dots that perfectly matched her hair. "Sorry. I guess I have some mothering instincts I didn't know about."

"You'll be a good one someday, so no need to practice on me."

Sage took a hard look at Emily. "You're not hurt."

"No."

"Well, you mentioned something about the ghost pushing you on the phone."

"Not me, Trevor. The ghost—a ghost, I'm not sure which one—touched me, but in a nice kind of way."

Sage's eyebrows shot up. "You have a lot to fill me in on. This time, do it slower and with more detail."

Emily led Sage to the kitchen and poured two generous glasses of iced tea. Once they were settled in at the table, Emily told Sage everything that had happened, pausing only to take long sips of tea. "So that's everything," she finally finished. "I feel so bad for Trevor and Mr. Williams."

"Let's talk about Trevor," Sage said firmly. "He is clearly being targeted by this ghost, like you said, even if things didn't get violent until today. The *HIM* spelled out on the table is especially concerning. It's like the ghost is explicitly calling him out, but why?"

"I know the most likely reason, and I'm trying really hard not to think about it," Emily said, her voice trembling.

"I don't want to think Trevor is involved in this, either. His energy feels a little off-balance, but the poor guy just gave up his life to come take care of a sick dad. My energy would be off, too."

Emily put up her hands and wiggled her fingers. "I don't sense any of this woo-woo energy stuff like you do, but Trevor doesn't strike me as the murderous type. Maybe the ghost recognizes that Trevor is Dillan's brother, and that's why she's lashing out at him."

"Maybe," Sage said doubtfully. "We haven't gotten far with séances, so I'm not even going to suggest that we try another one at this point. Keep talking to the ghost as you're walking around the house, though, and be honest with her. Tell her everything you know, and everything you suspect. Ask her to answer some questions in dreams. That seems to be her clearest method of communication."

Emily nodded in agreement. "We're missing something, Sage. I feel like my subconscious knows what it is, but it's not talking to my conscious brain."

"When the time is right, you'll find out what you need to know."

Emily just groaned. She never liked it when Sage gave such existential advice. No matter what the situation was or what words she used, it always boiled down to "just be patient." Emily did not sit and wait very well. "Thank you, oh wise one," she said sarcastically.

"I'm serious. You've had a hell of a week, Em. Go to

bed early tonight. Read a book. Drink a glass of wine. And whatever you do, stop thinking about the ghost and her body."

"Easier said than done."

"I know, but promise me you'll try. Give your brain a break. Sometimes, the harder you try to find an answer, the longer it takes."

"Here we go again." Emily made an exasperated face before smiling. She had to concede that Sage was right. Monday had been quiet, paranormally-speaking, and activity had only escalated again when Trevor showed up Tuesday morning. Now that Trevor was gone, it was likely Emily would have a quiet night and, hopefully, an equally quiet day on Wednesday. This was the perfect opportunity for her to think about anything but the fact that a murder victim was haunting her house.

Emily had been absolutely wrong about a quiet night at Eternal Rest.

The murdered woman's ghost had apparently taken Emily's invitation to share more information through dreams to heart, and Emily had woken up three times during the night. Each time, she found herself suddenly sitting straight up, gasping for breath as her hands grasped at her throat.

The first dream seemed to be a repeat of Rhonda's. Emily couldn't see anything other than a distant light and some shapes that were slightly darker than the rest of the void in front of her. She heard a man's angry voice say, "You don't deserve this fancy jewelry!" There was pressure against the back of her neck, and Emily could feel some-thing thin and hard digging into her skin. With a soft *pop*, the pressure disappeared, and Emily had a quick glimpse

163

of the gold necklace flying through the darkness before she woke up.

On top of feeling rattled by the vivid dream, Emily was also curious why the ghost would be showing her this memory. They had already found the necklace and identified it as hers. In fact, it was the necklace that had led them to the body. They had focused on the Clements plot because that was where the necklace was found. Otherwise, the sleeve of that letterman jacket would probably still be sticking out of the ground, unnoticed.

Eventually, Emily relaxed enough that she drifted off to sleep again. This time, the landscape of the dream was less dark. The shadows she had seen before were trees looming up in front of her. She was trying to run toward that distant light, but something was preventing her from moving forward, and a sharp tug on the tail of her shirt made her jerk backward. A second hand grabbed a fistful of hair near her scalp and yanked her head back.

"You trying to run for help? You'll never make it," the man's voice sneered into her ear. "They won't even hear you begging for your life."

Before she could react, the hands quickly let go and clamped around her neck. She twisted her body in an effort to break free, but the hands were too strong. A kick to the back of one knee made her fall backward, against the body of her attacker. He held her close, his breath hot against her cheek as she fought for air. The light began to waver as her vision blurred, and then everything went dark completely.

When Emily woke up this time, she was sweating. This was the dream she had experienced before, but this time it was so much more vivid. The memory of that voice and the dampness of the man's heavy breathing against her skin made her retch with horror and disgust. Emily threw back the covers and ran into the bathroom, but the sight of herself in the mirror helped her stomach settle. She was still herself, Emily Buchanan. She was alive and safe, and there wasn't a single mark on her neck. Emily stayed there for a long time, looking at herself in the mirror, watching herself take one shaky breath after another, reminding herself that what had happened in the dream hadn't actually happened to her.

Emily was afraid to go back to sleep after that. She took a book into the parlor and curled up on the sofa. As light began to grow in the sky, Emily fought the heaviness in her eyelids. She closed her eyes briefly and felt her head droop forward. With a jerk, she lifted her head again and blinked hard. She was exhausted, and she reasoned with herself that soon it would be time to get up and get breakfast ready for her guests, so she could let herself fall asleep for a little while. Surely she wouldn't dream in such a short span of time.

This time, when Emily's head dropped forward again, she didn't fight it. Her book tumbled from her limp hands and her body relaxed against the back of the sofa.

The third dream was the worst. As it began, there was no pain, and no one was hurting her this time. She was simply lying on the ground, staring up at a tangle of bare branches that allowed only a few stars to shine down onto her. Her eyelids fluttered and the world refused to come into focus. There was a sound that repeated over and over again, a scraping sound sometimes punctuated by a metallic clang. Emily tried to move her arms, but she was too weak to do anything more than twitch her hand. She could feel dirt beneath her fingers, which were cold now. Her throat ached when she tried to call for help, even though all that came out of her mouth was a quiet gurgling sound.

The scraping sound stopped, and Emily felt a hand against her throat again as a form loomed over her, blocking out the stars. "I guess I didn't finish the job the first time," the man's voice rumbled. He tightened his grip, bringing his second hand down to cover Emily's mouth and nose, completely cutting off her access to air. Emily's throat contracted as she fought weakly, and her lungs started to burn as she slowly suffocated. Her peripheral vision blinked out as she began to lose consciousness, and it seemed like a black curtain was being drawn over her eyes. The man leaned in so his face was just inches from hers, as if he wanted to make sure he was the last thing she ever saw.

She did see. Even in the darkness, even so close to death, she could see the handsome face of Trevor Williams, now twisted into a hateful, murderous visage.

This time when Emily woke up, she was crying. She rocked back and forth slowly, trying to soothe herself. The sun had risen over the horizon, but the growing brightness in the parlor didn't make her feel any better.

Overcome with horror and grief, Emily flopped down onto her side and drew her knees to her chest. She let the tears flow, burying her face against the cushion so her guests wouldn't hear her sobs. The dream had felt so real, and she had gotten a glimpse of the terror that woman had felt as she was dying. No, not a woman, Emily thought. A girl. Probably a teenager.

And she had been strangled and suffocated a second time, because her killer hadn't been thorough enough the first time.

Emily didn't need to imagine what it must have felt like to lie there on the ground, too weak to even get up and helpless to stop what was coming. She knew now that the scraping sound must have been a shovel, slowly digging the girl's grave.

Emily shuddered as she saw that face so close to hers again. This was the second time she had seen Trevor's face in a dream, and the ghost was clearly lashing out at him.

It wasn't even seven o'clock yet, but Emily called Sage anyway, praying she would wake up.

Sage answered on the third ring. "What, what's happening?" Sage said, her voice groggy.

When Emily tried to answer, she could feel tears welling up again. She fought to get out the word *dreams* without breaking down.

"Give me twenty minutes," Sage said, sounding more alert now. "Go start the coffee."

Emily was standing at the open front door when Sage arrived, and she quietly escorted her friend into the kitchen, closing the door before turning for a hug. As she felt Sage's arms around her, Emily sensed the tears coming again. She straightened up and wiped her eyes. "Sorry," she said. "I'm an emotional wreck this morning. These dreams, Sage. They felt so real. I know what it feels like to die."

Sage's eyes widened, but she stayed calm. "You sit while I pour. Tell me everything you experienced."

Emily didn't leave out a single detail. Sage was horrified, and just as concerned as Emily about Trevor's appearance in the dream. "I think we're right in assuming this girl was Dillan's girlfriend," Sage said. "So I suppose Trevor could have killed her, but why? And then what, he killed Dillan, too, or ran him out of town?"

"I don't know," Emily admitted. "I wish we could just ask him, but that might get a little awkward."

"Yeah, I don't think you're allowed to ask your employees questions like that."

The two women sat in silence for a while. Emily already felt a lot more calm, partly from sharing her experience but mostly from simply having her best friend there for support. "I'm sorry I got you out of bed so early," Emily said suddenly.

Sage waved her off. "You were right to call. Besides, Jen had already hit her snooze button twice, so you helped get her out of bed." While Sage was a night owl, her wife's job at the Oak Hill Chamber of Commerce required more normal hours.

"So what now?" Sage asked.

Emily frowned. "Normally I'd stay here at the house since I have guests, but I want to try to find out who this girl was. When I was looking through old newspapers for information about Dillan's disappearance, I didn't see anything about someone else going missing. Besides, if someone else from our school had gone missing, we would remember it."

Sage was nodding knowingly. "So she probably went to a different school, unless she was older than Dillan and had already graduated."

"Right. I want to go to the library over in Bulloch to look at their newspapers from the week after Dillan disappeared. Maybe she came from there."

"I say go for it. Your guests can live without you for a few hours."

As a matter of fact, Emily's guests were more than understanding about her plan to be away from the house for a while: they were downright enthusiastic. They had gotten wind of the news about the body in the cemetery the day before, and they were absolutely fascinated to be staying at a bed and breakfast so closely tied to a murder case. Mrs. Morgan made Emily promise to share anything she discovered in her research.

Once the family had left for their day's activities, Emily made the drive to Bulloch. It was on the opposite side of Oak Hill from Eternal Rest, so it took half an hour to reach the downtown library. Like Oak Hill, Bulloch had a well-kept historic square that was popular with day-trippers and people looking to get out of Atlanta for a quiet weekend.

Soon, Emily was anxiously scrolling through the microfiche files for the *Bulloch Bee* from the days after Dillan's disappearance. Two hours later, she was still scrolling, and she was about to conclude that the girl must have come from somewhere else. Then Emily's eye caught a small sub-headline in the police blotter: "Teen Reported Missing." There was only one line under it, reading, "Kelly Stern, 17, has been reported missing since October 1, and any information of her whereabouts should be reported to the Bulloch Police Department."

That was it. No in-depth articles like Dillan had received. No reports of a massive search by community volunteers. Just one single line in the back of the local section of the newspaper.

Emily sat back, her hands pressed to her cheeks as if she could physically keep the tears she felt in her eyes from spilling over. She knew this was the girl whose body they had found. The timing of the disappearance and the girl's age fit so perfectly with Dillan's own story. She must have been his girlfriend.

Emily printed off a copy of the page and walked outside. The sunshine felt out of place, as if the weather should have reflected Emily's somber mood. She immediately pulled out her phone and dialed the Oak Hill Police Department. She asked for Roger and waited impatiently on hold until he picked up.

"Roger? Hi, it's Emily, from Eternal Rest. I know who the girl is. The girl we found in the cemetery."

Roger expressed surprise when Emily filled him in, but he told her to get to the station immediately so they could discuss what she'd found. Emily promised she was on her way, and then she called Trevor before she could lose her courage.

When he answered, Emily took a deep breath and reminded herself to speak calmly. "Trevor, hi. Um, did your brother have a girlfriend?"

Trevor was quiet for a long time. Emily actually pulled the phone away from her ear to glance at the screen, assuring herself that the call was still connected. Finally, Trevor sighed. He spoke slowly, carefully. "I knew Dillan had something going on, but he was really secretive about it. When he disappeared, I thought that was why he had been acting so oddly. I figured he had been making plans to leave town for a while. He didn't want to live in Oak Hill for the rest of his life. But he had never mentioned a girlfriend to me. I know what it looks like, Emily. The police have even told us that they suspect Dillan killed that woman you found, but I don't believe it."

Emily bit her lip, her mind going back to her dream, and that vision of Trevor's twisted face glaring down at her as she died. Obviously, the police didn't suspect Trevor. Emily, on the other hand, could feel fear rising in her again, and she felt a little short of breath.

It's just nerves, she told herself.

Emily wanted to trust Trevor, but it seemed like the ghost kept telling her not to. She didn't say a word about Kelly Stern. Instead, she asked gently about how Mr. Williams was taking the news.

"He's upset, I'm sure, but he's never been great about sharing his feelings," Trevor said. "He's so worn out from this week's chemo that I'm not even sure he's got the energy to process all of this properly."

A sudden wave of guilt washed over Emily. If only they hadn't pulled on that jacket sleeve. If only they hadn't continued asking the ghost to communicate with them.

No, not "the ghost." She had a name. She had once been a living, breathing human being, and someone had killed her, buried her, and fled. If they could help find answers and hopefully, justice, then that was right. It would bring an unfathomable amount of pain to the Williams family, but if Dillan could be tracked down and the truth extracted from him, then it would at least bring peace to the ghost of Kelly Stern.

"Well, give him my best," Emily said finally. "And you take care, too. See you tomorrow."

Emily thought about Trevor for the entire drive to the police station, alternating between dread at learning what role he had played in Kelly's murder and sympathy that he and his dad were having to process such painful revelations.

Roger greeted Emily warmly when she arrived at the pretty two-story brick building that had been home to the Oak Hill Police Department for nearly a century. The inside was all modern, but the outside still fit in seamlessly with the other historic buildings on the square.

"Let's see what you've got," Roger said as Emily held up the copy of the newspaper page. She quickly told him about her thought that the body was from somewhere other than Oak Hill as Roger nodded. "We thought the same, but you've gotten to the research phase much faster than our team."

He put the paper down and looked at her sternly, one elbow propped on his desk so he could easily point at Emily. "You are not to share this information with anyone, under any circumstances," he said. "There is zero evidence at this point that there is any connection between this girl" —he stopped pointing long enough to tap the paper with his finger—"and the body in your cemetery."

"Understood," Emily said, feeling a little like a chastised child.

"However," Roger continued, finally relaxing his arm and sitting back, "I really appreciate you doing this leg work. We'll see if we can track down her family today.

Hopefully they still live in the Bulloch area. Give me a call in a few days, and we'll catch up with each other."

Emily agreed, and as she stood to go, Roger gave her one more warning. "Not a word, Miss Emily, especially not to that Williams boy who works for you."

No, you definitely don't have to worry about that.

Sage's shop was in a little office building just two streets over from the square. It had been built in the 1930s, so the white plaster facade had an Art Deco style. Seeing Beyond was on the second floor, and Sage had decorated the place to look a lot less like a business and more like a Victorian sitting room. Every time she was there, Emily was reminded that one of the reasons she and Sage were such good friends was because of their shared appreciation for that era's beautiful furnishings.

The standard cream-colored carpet, a generic staple of so many offices, only showed in a few places because Sage had made such copious use of dark-toned throw rugs. A carved Victorian sofa had been reupholstered in a rich midnight-blue velvet, and matching curtains covered the windows. A little cubby on one side of the office had been created by installing tall, crammed-full bookshelves arranged in a U-shape around the wall. A curtain hung from a rod suspended between two of the bookshelves, but this one was a gold brocade with tiny glass beads sewn onto it in a swirling pattern.

As Emily walked into Seeing Beyond, Sage was just opening the gold curtain. She was followed out by an elderly woman who thanked her profusely before leaving. As soon as the door closed behind the woman, Sage turned expectantly to Emily. "If you're here, that means you found something!"

Emily filled Sage in on her luck at the Bulloch library, and they both agreed that Kelly Stern was likely the victim. "That helps us," Sage said. "Now, when we try to communicate with the ghost, we can call her by her name. We have a more personal connection to rely on."

"I don't know if I feel comfortable doing a séance at the house tonight. I've got a big family in, and I'm not sure I want to risk scaring the hell out of them. They're here for a relaxing family getaway, not a ghost hunt."

"I don't want to do a séance at the house." One corner of Sage's mouth turned up in a smile. "I want to do a séance in the cemetery!"

23

Emily had been reluctant to agree to a séance that night, even if it was in the cemetery. When Sage suggested that trying to communicate with the ghost again might prevent Emily from seeing more of Kelly's memories in her dreams, she gave in.

This time, it would be just Sage and Emily. Inviting Trevor was out of the question, and Sage had decided to leave Reed out, too, since Kelly might be more willing to talk if it was just two women conducting the séance. "It will be like a girls' night," Sage said optimistically.

Emily forewarned her guests that she would be out at the cemetery for a while, and they made her promise to fill them in the next morning at breakfast.

At nine o'clock, Sage arrived, and she and Emily walked to the cemetery. It was a darker night than usual. Clouds had moved in, covering the sliver of moon that had risen shortly after sunset. There was a light breeze, and Emily felt a slight chill even though she had bundled up in a jacket.

The Clements plot still gave off an unsettled feeling. Its state of disarray, with the overturned earth of the filled-in grave, the dismantled wall, and the pile of old bricks, mirrored Emily's thoughts. One moment she felt sympathy for Kelly, the next suspicion about both Dillan and Trevor.

And over all of it, like a constant buzz running through every thought, was a growing fear. Emily wasn't even sure what she was afraid of, but the closer they got to the Clements plot, the more her brain tried to tell her feet to turn around and leave.

Sage seemed to feel the underlying sense of dread, too, and she kept moving her head back and forth as she and Emily sat down on the pathway in front of the Clements plot. Whether she was looking for ghosts or living people, Emily wasn't sure.

Quickly, Sage pulled a candle and her paper and pencil out of her bag. Since Kelly seemed to prefer writing to communicate, it didn't seem worth bringing out the bell or the silver dollar that would ordinarily be a part of her tools.

Once the candle was lit, Sage instantly began calling Kelly's name. "We want to communicate with you, Kelly Stern. Are you here? If you are, you can write through me like you did before. Or you can talk to us, or make a noise. Can you give us a sign?"

A brick on top of the pile toppled off, landing on the ground with a soft thud.

Emily turned to Sage, her eyes wide. "Was that a sign?"

"I don't think it was the breeze. This is good. She always took so long to come out and communicate in our previous séances. Knowing her name is helping, I think."

Sage raised her voice to speak to Kelly again, but she kept a comforting, almost parental tone as she said, "Thank you, Kelly. Emily found out about you today from a newspaper article. We are so sorry that your soul is still here. We want to help you find peace. I'm going to ask you questions, and I want you to make a sound one time for yes, or twice for no. Do you understand?"

For a moment there was only silence, then a distinct tap sounded from somewhere in front of them. It sounded like someone had struck one of the Clements headstones with a stick.

"Wonderful!" Sage said, her voice overly enthusiastic as she tried to encourage Kelly. "You're doing great! Kelly, do you know who killed you?"

Another tap sounded almost immediately.

"Did Dillan Williams kill you?"

Two taps.

Instead of relief, Emily only felt dread, and she clasped her hands together nervously. She knew what question Sage would ask next, and she was afraid Kelly's answer would be a single tap.

"Did Trevor Williams kill you?" Sage asked.

The question was met with silence. Emily could feel a tightness in her chest as she anticipated the answer, leaning forward slightly as if it could help her hear better. She held her breath.

There was a quiet crunch that came from somewhere ahead and to the left. Just one.

Emily's hands flew to her mouth, and she could feel her fingers trembling against her lips. "Oh, my God," she breathed. "It's him."

"I don't know if that was Kelly answering us," Sage whispered. "That sounded like someone stepping on a branch."

Emily and Sage both fell silent, listening now not for a ghost but for the sound of someone in the cemetery with them. They heard nothing but the faint rattle of the breeze moving through the cemetery.

Their eyes were directed to the area the sound had come from, the same place where Emily had seen the shadowed form walking toward her during the EVP session with Nathan and Brianne. It was too dark to see anything outside the shine of the candle, and Emily was wrestling with whether or not to turn on her flashlight when there was a quiet noise right in front of them.

It was the pencil, rolling slowly toward Sage. With a gasp, Sage snatched the pencil up and said, "I'm ready."

Her hand began to fly across the top sheet of paper as soon as she set the lead point against it. Even with so little illumination, Emily could easily read the words that spread across the page, repeated again and again in large, bold letters.

He's here. He's here. He's here. He's here.

Emily was on her feet with her flashlight pointing toward the sound they had heard before Sage had even stopped writing. Despite her fear, she ran forward. "Where are you?" she shouted. "Trevor, I know you're there. Come out!"

Briefly, Emily realized she was taking a huge risk. If Trevor had killed Kelly, he might kill Emily without hesitation, too. At the moment, though, she wanted answers more than security.

There was a sharp intake of breath to her left, and Emily swung her flashlight around. There was a big holly bush where the sound had come from. "I know you're there!"

"Okay," Trevor's voice came from behind the bush. "Don't hurt me."

That seemed like an odd thing for him to say, but when he walked out to face Emily, he had both hands up, as if she was pointing a gun at him instead of a flashlight.

"Sage, call the police right now!" Emily called over her shoulder.

"No, please!" Trevor took a step forward, and Emily

shrank back. "Please, we're only here to look for more evidence! We didn't know you'd be out here, too."

"We?"

Trevor sighed. His arms drooped to his sides and he hung his head as if he was exhausted. "Me and Dillan," he said quietly. "He's here."

The ghost's words echoed in Emily's mind.

But Kelly had also indicated that Dillan hadn't killed her. And if Trevor had, then why would he be there with his brother? Also, Dillan had been missing for the past seventeen years, so how was he suddenly here, in the cemetery?

Emily didn't understand, and she said as much to Trevor.

By now, Sage was standing at Emily's side, her phone in her hand. "So am I calling the cops, or what?" She sounded more curious than scared.

"Please don't," Trevor said. "If anything, we would just get in trouble for trespassing, but Dillan doesn't want anyone to know he's back yet."

Emily nodded curtly. "Fine. We'll hear you out. Tell us why you killed Kelly Stern."

Trevor's eyebrows knitted together, and he shook his head disbelievingly. "You really think I killed her?" Emily noticed that he didn't ask who Kelly was. He already seemed to know the name belonged to the body they had found.

"Dillan, they know you're here already," Trevor called. "You may as well come help me tell them what happened."

There were the sounds of footsteps in the dry grass behind Trevor, and a man who looked very unlike the Dillan Williams Emily had known in high school emerged from the shadows. He was still tall and well-built, but less muscular than he had been in his days of being a home-town football star. He had grown a thick beard, too, and his dark-blond hair was a little longer. The only part of him that looked familiar were his green eyes, which seemed to glow in the flashlight's beam.

"Hi, Emily, Sage." Dillan's voice was deep but quiet.

"Okay, go sit right there." Emily pointed to a nearby plot that had a bench on it. Trevor and Dillan complied, and Emily stood in front of them once they were seated. She lowered the flashlight enough that she wouldn't blind them with its light. Sage stood to the side, apparently happy to let Emily handle communicating with the living. "Talk."

Trevor and Dillan exchanged glances, and Trevor gave his brother a small nod. "Emily wants to know the truth, too," he said. "You can trust her."

Dillan stared down at his hands for a while, his fingers twisting as if he were trying to untangle an invisible knot. When he began to speak, it was in the same quiet voice. "Kelly and I had been dating for about eight months," he said. "I was in love with her, but I couldn't tell anyone we were together. She was… she wasn't from a very good family. Her mom was an alcoholic, and her stepdad sometimes hit her." Dillan glanced over at Trevor. "Dad would have never let me keep dating her if he found out."

"He didn't even tell me he had a girlfriend," Trevor said. "What I said to you on the phone yesterday was true, Emily."

"Kelly wanted us to leave town together," Dillan continued. "She kept talking about how we'd just drive and find somewhere else to start a new life. I kept telling her that we needed to wait. I wanted to get the hell out of here, too, but I thought we should at least wait until graduation. Kelly's home life was so much worse than mine, though, and the idea of waiting a couple of years was unbearable for her.

"We used to come out here to the cemetery a lot. Even

if other kids were out here, it was easy to find a dark corner where no one would see us together. I would pick her up on the edge of Bulloch—never at her house—and we'd drive out here or to another one of our favorite spots."

Dillan paused as his eyes focused somewhere behind Emily. "We got in such a huge fight that night. She said we should either leave town immediately or tell everyone we were dating. She thought that if people knew she was dating me, it would somehow make things easier for her. She had always hated having to hide our relationship, but she started to think of it as some kind of magic solution that would keep her safe from her mom and stepdad. I kept telling her I wasn't ready to do either one of those things, and she got more and more angry with me."

Dillan's voice broke. "I left her. I just walked away and left here standing here alone, in the dark. She was crying. I got in my car and started driving all over the backroads, just so angry and frustrated. I loved her, but I just wasn't ready for those things. I should have agreed to tell everyone about us. It wouldn't have fixed Kelly's life, but it wouldn't have hurt anyone." Dillan leaned forward and put his face in his hands. Emily couldn't hear him crying, but she could see his shoulders shaking. Trevor put a supportive arm around his brother.

Emily wanted to shout at him to keep talking, because they were so close to knowing what had happened that night. Dillan's grief seemed genuine, though, and she knew he needed time to collect himself. Eventually, he continued, but he avoided meeting anyone's eyes. "I came back a little while later, maybe after half an hour or so. I was angry, but I wasn't going to leave her stranded in the cemetery all night. I called her name again and again, and when she didn't answer I figured she was still too mad to even respond to me. I kept walking through the cemetery, and I nearly tripped over her because I didn't see her in the dark. She was lying on the ground. I shook her and shook her, but she didn't move. I had a lighter in my pocket, so I used it to see her better. There were these awful red marks around her neck, and I knew someone had"—Dillan swallowed hard—"had strangled her. I panicked, and I just ran away. I got in my car, and I drove as far away as I could."

Dillan fell silent, and Emily's eyes flicked to Trevor. His gaze, though, was on his big brother, his expression sad. When Dillan didn't start talking again, Trevor took up the thread. "By the time Dillan calmed down enough to think clearly, he realized he would be a suspect if he went back and told the police."

"So I just kept driving," Dillan said. "After a few years of bouncing from town to town, I finally settled down in Virginia. It wasn't until about five years ago that I tracked down Trevor and sent him an email, though I asked him not to tell the rest of the family we were in touch. I didn't write anything about Kelly, but I assumed the murder would be the first thing he asked me about, since I left town the same night she was killed. When Trevor never mentioned it, I realized someone must have covered it up. Now, of course, we know they just buried her here. As far as I can figure, I must have come back here while her killer was getting a shovel to dig her grave with. If I'd waited, I could have caught him."

And if he'd waited, Emily thought, he might have realized that Kelly wasn't dead yet, but simply unconscious.

"So then who killed her?" Emily nearly shouted the question in her frustration.

Dillan shrugged. "I don't know. Her stepdad, maybe. Or some other kid who was sneaking into the cemetery at night. I hate that we'll never find out. It's bad enough that Kelly is dead because of me, but knowing that I also missed the chance to catch the person makes it even worse."

"It was you that I saw in the cemetery last Friday night." It wasn't even a question.

"Yeah," Dillan admitted. "I've been coming out here at night, or really early in the morning, hoping to find some answers. Sometimes Trevor comes with me."

"Thanks for nearly giving me a heart attack that night. How long have you been back in Oak Hill, anyway?"

"As long as Trevor. When he said he was coming back, I felt like I should, too. It's past time for me to deal with what happened that night. I managed to get here, but I just haven't been ready to face the people in this town yet. I've been staying at one of the motels out by the interstate, trying to get up my courage."

Emily looked over to Sage, who just returned the look with one raised eyebrow. "Well?" Sage prompted. "What does your intuition say now?"

"I believe them," Emily said quietly. She turned to face the two brothers, who were now looking at her expectantly. "But I would sure like to know who actually murdered Kelly. If it wasn't one of them, then why has she been trying to hurt Trevor and showing him to me in my dreams?"

"What?" Trevor looked surprised.

Emily nodded. "I've been seeing Kelly's memories through dreams. Her last moments. I've only actually seen her killer's face twice now, and both times it's been you, Trevor."

Trevor jerked back as if Emily had physically struck him. "But it's not. It wasn't. I didn't even know about her until they found the body. When I told Dillan about it, he realized it was Kelly and told me everything."

"Calm down, Trevor," Sage said firmly. "Em isn't

183

accusing you. She's trying to figure out why the ghost seems to be pointing its finger at you."

"Trevor was only fifteen back then," Dillan said sadly. "Just a kid. It wasn't fair of me to abandon him like I did."

Emily gasped. Of course Trevor had only been a teenager at the time, so why had she seen Trevor in her dreams as he was now, an adult? The pieces suddenly fell into place, and Emily felt a wave of dizziness. She reached out a hand to Sage to help steady herself. Emily whispered the words, but they carried to Dillan and Trevor, who both stared at her with shocked expressions.

"Mr. Williams killed Kelly."

24

"It makes sense," Emily said, talking quickly in an effort to sort out all the details flying through her mind. "I saw that wedding photo of your parents, on the wall in your living room, and I noticed how much you look like your dad, Trevor. Kelly's ghost may not be able to differentiate between you as you look now and your dad as he looked back then. She's mistaking you for your dad."

Dillan was running his hands through his hair, thinking. "I've actually suspected him before," he said carefully, "but never with any real conviction. I don't know if I can really buy my dad killing someone. What reason would he have?"

"He must have known about her," Trevor said. "After you disappeared and everyone gave up searching, Dad would actually get angry if people brought up your name. He'd rant about how you were supposed to take over the family business one day. It was like even though we all knew you might be dead, he was still mad that you'd ignored your responsibilities."

Dillan and Trevor suddenly looked a lot like the teenagers they had been on that night, young and sort of lost. Emily wished there was something she could say to make them feel better, but instead she said sadly, "I think it's time we called the police."

Sage already had the phone to her ear by the time Emily looked over at her. She must have had the number already typed in and ready to go. She spoke rapidly to the person who picked up, telling them their suspicions about Mr. Williams. Emily wasn't sure it would do any good when it was truly just a hunch based on the word of a ghost, and she wished it was earlier in the day, when Roger would have still been on duty. Whoever was answering the phone this late at night probably didn't know much about the case and wouldn't take their news about Mr. Williams seriously.

"They said they'd send a car around to his house," Sage said when she was done. "I don't think they're ready to make any big arrest based solely on what I just said."

"I think we should all go to the police station," said Emily. She turned to Dillan. "Even you. I know you don't want to, but the longer you wait to come forward, the more people are going to think you were involved in Kelly's death."

Dillan looked uncomfortable with the suggestion, but he agreed that Emily had a point. Together, they walked toward the cemetery entrance. Trevor had parked on the side of the cemetery opposite Eternal Rest, where his car might go unnoticed, so when they reached the front gate, Emily turned to tell him they would meet up again at the police station. Her eyes flicked toward movement to the left of the gate.

"Get down!" Emily yelled the words in the second before the shotgun fired. Luckily, Trevor and Dillan reacted immediately, ducking down to avoid the shot that had been fired in their direction. Mr. Williams was stalking toward the gate, and he prepared to take another shot.

"I knew it!" He was shouting, and there was no sign of the weak old man he had been the last couple of times Emily saw him. At the moment, the adrenaline and anger coursing through him were giving him an uncanny vitality. "I knew you were back! When Trevor snuck out tonight, I knew exactly where he was going, and I knew exactly who he'd be with. When you disappeared seventeen years ago, I decided I'd shoot you myself if you were ever dumb enough to come back."

Emily was half-crouched behind a headstone, ready to duck if Mr. Williams fired again, but Trevor and Dillan were still in the middle of the pathway, ready targets for their father. Glancing around wildly, Emily spotted Sage, who was crawling carefully between headstones. Emily could faintly see a glow near one ear, and she knew Sage was on the phone with the police again.

If we can just keep him talking, we'll be okay.

"Mr. Williams," she called, her voice sounding small to her ears, "they're your sons. Please don't do this."

"They're not my sons," Mr. Williams sneered. "Not anymore. That one"—he pointed at Dillan—"gave up being a part of this family back when he decided he'd rather run away instead of acting like a responsible adult. And the other one claimed he was coming back to town to take care of me, but obviously he was here for his brother."

Mr. Williams's face was twisted with hate and rage, and Emily recognized the expression from the dream where she had been both strangled and suffocated. He was looking at Dillan again, his voice cracking as he shouted. "You had obligations to this family! Your whole life, I had planned to give the business to you one day. Your whole life, I taught you about the value of reputation, of power within the community. You were supposed to marry a good girl from Oak Hill and continue all the hard work that your grandfather and I had started. But no, you had to be the rebellious one. When I found out about that trash you were supposedly in love with, I knew it was over for you. She was ruining everything I had ever done for you."

Dillan was shaking his head vehemently. "No! She wanted us to have a better life together. One where we were free from families like ours. We really did love each other."

"And yet you're the reason she's dead! You left her here in the cemetery by herself, and all I had to do was sneak up behind her. You call that love?"

Dillan made a sound in his throat like a wild animal. Mr. Williams had relaxed his grip on the shotgun, but now he tightened his hold and pointed it directly at Dillan's chest.

Distract him! Emily's brain was shouting. She asked the question that had been on her mind since being told the body wasn't Dillan's. "Kelly was buried wearing Dillan's letterman jacket, but she wasn't wearing it when you killed her, was she?"

Mr. Williams sneered at Emily. "No! I found it on the ground, and I put it on her. That way, if the body was ever discovered, it would look like Dillan had killed her. Of course, he wouldn't even have been around to claim he was innocent since he's a coward who runs away from responsibilities."

Dillan jerked as if he was going to lunge at his father, and Mr. Williams quickly swiveled his head toward his son again. Emily started shouting more questions at him. "What are you going to do? Shoot and kill all of us? Are you going to dig graves for all of us, like you did for Kelly?"

Mr. Williams rounded on Emily. "You could have avoided all of this," he hissed. "When Trevor told me he was going to be working out here, I thought for sure Dillan was staying at your weird little place. I thought you were helping them reconnect. But when I came out here to see, it was obvious you knew nothing about it. Just a coincidence. You should be in that house right now, not out here in the middle of it."

Emily's fear evaporated as her anger grew, and she stood up to her full height. "Shut the hell up, Mr. Williams. You killed an innocent girl in my cemetery. You better believe I'm in the middle of it."

A few leaves tumbled down the pathway toward Mr. Williams, gaining speed as they went. Emily could feel a rush of wind whipping her ponytail. With a wail, Mr. Williams sailed backward, his shotgun flying into the grass as he landed hard on his back.

Dillan and Trevor were instantly on their feet. Trevor snatched up the shotgun and trained it on his father while Dillan simply straddled Mr. Williams's chest, pinning his arms in place and keeping him prone.

The police arrived three minutes later, utterly astonished at the strange family scene before them.

By the time the police got Mr. Williams on his feet, he had turned into a weak, sick old man again, his energy spent. His face was still contorted with anger, but he needed help getting up and had to lean heavily on the officer who put him in handcuffs. After everything he had said and done in front of four witnesses, Mr. Williams didn't even try to deny that he had killed Kelly Stern or that he had just attempted to kill his eldest son.

Emily and Sage spent hours at the police station. Dillan and Trevor were still there when the two women were finally told to go home and get some rest. Even Roger had come in to help oversee all the questioning, reporting, and confessing that was happening.

Sage hugged Emily tightly in the parking lot before they went their separate ways, but neither one spoke much.

They were too exhausted, both physically and mentally, to talk about everything that had happened. The only thing Emily said was, "I don't think Trevor is going to want to work for me anymore."

"I'll help you find someone new," Sage promised, punctuating her statement with a yawn.

Emily drove home on autopilot, her eyes barely able to focus on the road ahead. She clicked off her headlights as she turned into her driveway, not wanting to wake up her guests.

Five minutes later, Emily was in bed and fast asleep. She had no dreams of dying.

Emily actually woke up before her alarm. She still felt exhausted, but her brain was racing, and she knew she wouldn't be able to go back to sleep. She rolled out of bed and got dressed, not motivated enough to attempt doing her hair or makeup. She was sure her guests would excuse her disheveled appearance when they got a firsthand account of what was guaranteed to be the only thing anyone in Oak Hill was discussing that day.

It was a shame Dillan had come back to town only to find out his father was a murderer. Now that Kelly's story had finally been told, Emily assumed Dillan would return to Virginia. Emily wondered idly if he had a wife and kids in his new life. Trevor would probably head back to Atlanta.

Emily got through three cups of coffee before both her cell phone and the Eternal Rest phone started ringing every few minutes. Even *The Oak Hill Monitor* called, looking for a quote.

As she had expected, the family staying at Eternal Rest was thrilled to be at the center of the activity. They actually expressed disappointment that they were checking out and heading to their respective homes that morning. Emily was disappointed, too, simply because it meant she had to clean the rooms and get the house ready for the new guests checking in that afternoon. What she wanted more than anything was a day off.

Sage arrived around nine, looking a lot more perky than Emily. "I thought I'd stop by before opening up the shop," Sage said. "I want to see if we can get Kelly to cross over."

"You might have a hard time hearing any knocks or anything," Emily answered. "The guests are all still here. They just finished breakfast and went back upstairs."

"We're sticking with writing," Sage said. "Dreams and writing seem to be Kelly's go-to methods of communication."

"And trying to hurt the person who hurt her. Or who she thought hurt her. Poor Trevor. I guess she really was trying to get revenge with the exploding microwave."

"At least she helped diffuse the situation with Mr. Williams last night! That wave of energy she conjured was impressive."

Emily sobered. "What's going to happen to him, Sage? He's a murderer, but that doesn't change the fact that he's dying."

"He's dying. That doesn't change the fact that he's a murderer," countered Sage. She spread her hands. "I don't know. House arrest, maybe? Either way, I don't think he'll be running his construction business or visiting friends around town anymore."

"And to think I felt so sorry for him," Emily said, putting her hands on her hips and shaking her head. "My intuition did not come through for me there."

Sage shrugged as she began walking toward the dining room. "You're learning."

"I need to find a ghost that communicates by email," Emily said, following Sage and dropping into a chair. She laid her head down on the table for a moment, her eyes closed. She was exhausted but happy they had been able to help a ghost and, hopefully, bring some closure to Kelly's family. Roger had mentioned during their time at the police station that Kelly's mother still lived in Bulloch.

"Let's get started," Sage said briskly. "I've got a client coming in right at ten."

Emily sat up and saw that Sage had already put a single sheet of paper and a pencil on the table. When Emily asked where the candle was, Sage said, "You know, we were in such a hurry last night that we left everything sitting out there at the Clements plot. If you can grab it all for me later, I'd appreciate it."

"Of course." Emily smiled at Sage. "Thank you for all of your help in this."

"You know I enjoyed it." Sage turned her head to a spot on the ceiling as she took up the pencil. "Kelly Stern, the man who killed you has been caught. You helped us catch him last night when you pushed him over. What a brave girl you are! You saved all of our lives last night. Now that you can be at peace, you can let yourself move on to the next phase of your journey. Do you see a light, Kelly? I want you to walk toward it."

Sage's hand twitched, and when it stopped moving there were two capital letters on the page: *NO.*

"You don't want to go home?"

The writing wasn't as fast this time, but the pencil still formed bold, insistent letters that said, "I am home."

Emily was surprised, but she smiled at the empty air. "You want to stay here, at Eternal Rest?"

Yes, Sage wrote. *Stay. Help.*

Now Emily was beaming. "I would love that!" she said. "You will always be welcome in my home. And Sage is here every month for a séance, so you can talk to her then."

Sage's hand was still, but she was smiling. "Well, that's settled," she said, turning to Emily. "You have another resident at Eternal Rest."

Instead of calling like so many other people in Oak Hill, Reed simply dropped by at the end of his lunch break. He had found Sage's candle, paper, and pencil on the brick path by the Clements plot, and Emily suspected that returning them was an excuse to visit so he could hear about the biggest Oak Hill scandal in years.

Reed had handed over Sage's things wordlessly, but his expression was clearly asking for details. Emily waved him in, and they settled at the kitchen table so she could tell him everything that had transpired. When she was done, Reed looked at Emily seriously. "I sure hope he didn't damage any headstones with that shotgun."

"Really? That's your concern? We could have been killed last night."

Reed held up a finger. "But you weren't. And since you're all safe, I can worry about my headstones."

Emily laughed, and it felt good to have a little humor after such somber events. "The next time you have a box of things you found around the cemetery, Reed, give it to someone else."

Reed just smiled wickedly. "You're going to thank me when word of this hits bigger news outlets than our humble little town paper. It's going to bring a lot of people to Eternal Rest."

"I hope you're right. I need money for a new roof."

"That's the spirit." Reed rose, but his smile faded as he looked down at Emily and put a hand on her shoulder. "I'm glad you're okay, Emily," he said earnestly.

Emily reached up and gave his hand a squeeze. "Thanks, Reed."

No sooner had Reed left than the doorbell rang. The first two guests had arrived. Emily got them checked in, chatting cheerfully with them about where they came from and what they planned to do during their time at Eternal Rest. It felt so delightfully normal.

As her guests went upstairs to settle in, Emily went back to the kitchen to get yet another cup of coffee. It was the one thing keeping her from giving in and taking a nap.

As Emily refilled her cup, she heard the distinct sound of something hitting the floor. She whirled around and saw the pencil coming to a stop after apparently rolling off the table. Emily's eyes flicked up to the paper, and she saw two words written there: *He's here.*

The writing wasn't large and urgent like Kelly's previous messages. It was small and simple and straightforward.

Emily gasped.

"Scott?"

A NOTE FROM THE AUTHOR

Thank you for reading *Sweet Dreams*! I'm really excited about this new series and the chance to get to know a whole new cast of characters. I hope you'll join me on the journey as Emily continues to search for Scott's ghost and, of course, as more mysteries need to be solved. But first, will you please leave a review for this book? Your reviews mean so much to indie authors like me, because it helps me keep doing what I love, which is telling stories.

Thank you,

Beth

NEXT IN THE SERIES

Find out what's next for Emily, Sage, and the ghosts
of Eternal Rest Bed and Breakfast!

Late Checkout

ETERNAL REST BED AND BREAKFAST BOOK TWO
PARANORMAL COZY MYSTERIES

One of the new guests at Eternal Rest Bed and Breakfast is
a real jerk—even one of the ghosts says so. Emily
Buchanan's patience is put to the test by the entitled,
uptight investor who owns the abandoned hotel on the
edge of town. Jaxon Knight-MacGinn's plans to revamp
the hotel into an expensive resort is stirring up a lot of
resentment around Oak Hill, and no one seems all that
upset when he turns up dead. Even Jaxon's business
partner seems content to carry on without him. There are
plenty of suspects among the living, but it's the ghosts who
have the most clues about the murder. As even Emily
herself becomes a suspect, she also has to grapple with a
shocking revelation about her late husband's spirit.

BOOKS BY BETH DOLGNER

The Eternal Rest Bed and Breakfast Series
Paranormal Cozy Mystery
Sweet Dreams
Late Checkout (September 2021)
Picture Perfect (December 2021)

The Betty Boo, Ghost Hunter Series
Paranormal Romance
Ghost of a Threat
Ghost of a Whisper
Ghost of a Memory
Ghost of a Hope

Manifest
Young Adult Steampunk

A Talent for Death
Young Adult Urban Fantasy

Non-fiction
Georgia Spirits and Specters
Everyday Voodoo

ABOUT THE AUTHOR

Beth Dolgner writes paranormal fiction and non-fiction. Her interest in things that go bump in the night really took off on a trip to Savannah, Georgia, so it's fitting that the Betty Boo, Ghost Hunter series of paranormal romance novels takes place in that spooky city. Beth's first book was the non-fiction *Georgia Spirits and Specters*, which is a collection of Georgia ghost stories.

Since Georgia is obviously on her mind, you might think Beth lives there. Well, she did, but these days she and her husband live in Berlin, Germany, with their three cats. Beth misses those mild Georgia winters and proper iced tea, but there's no reason her characters can't enjoy those things.

Beth also enjoys giving presentations on Victorian death and mourning traditions as well as Victorian Spiritualism. She has been a volunteer at an historic cemetery, a ghost tour guide and a paranormal investigator. Right now she's chronicling the best spooky spots around Europe.

Keep up with Beth and sign up for her newsletter at Beth-Dolgner.com.

Printed in Great Britain
by Amazon

30171970R00118